A SERIES OF UNFORTUNATE EVENTS

THE H

This book is the only one existing which describes every last detail of the Baudelaire orphans' miserable stay at Heimlich Hospital. There are many pleasant things to read about in the world, but this book contains none of them. Instead, it contains such burdensome details as a suspicious shopkeeper, unnecessary surgery, an intercom system, anesthesia, heart-shaped balloons, and some very startling news about a fire. Clearly you do not want to read about these things, and this book is best left on the ground, where you undoubtedly found it . . .

A SERIES OF UNFORTUNATE EVENTS

THE HOSTILE HOSPITAL

Lemony Snicket

Illustrated by Brett Helquist

First published in Great Britain 2003
by
Egmont Books Ltd
This Large Print edition published by
BBC Audiobooks Ltd
by arrangement with
Egmont Books Ltd
2004

ISBN 0 7540 7904 X

British Library Cataloguing in Publication Data

Snicket, Lemony
 The hostile hospital. —Large print ed.—(A series of
 unfortunate events ; bk. 8)
 1. Baudelaire, Klaus (Fictitious character)—Juvenile
 fiction 2. Baudelaire, Sunny (Fictitious character)
 —Juvenile fiction 3. Baudelaire, Violet (Fictitious
 character)—Juvenile fiction 4. Orphans—Juvenile
 fiction 5. Brothers and sisters—Juvenile fiction
 6. Humorous stories 7. Children's stories
 8. Large type books
 I. Title II. Helquist, Brett
 813. 5'4[J]

ISBN 0-7540-7904-X

Printed and bound in Great Britain by
Antony Rowe Ltd., Chippenham, Wiltshire

For Beatrice—
Summer without you is as cold
as winter.
Winter without you is even colder.

CHAPTER ONE

There are two reasons why a writer would end a sentence with the word 'stop' written entirely in capital letters STOP. The first is if the writer were writing a telegram, which is a coded message sent through an electrical wire STOP. In a telegram, the word 'stop' in all capital letters is the code for the end of a sentence STOP. But there is another reason why a writer would end a sentence with 'stop' written entirely in capital letters, and that is to warn readers that the book they are reading is so utterly wretched that if they have begun reading it, the best thing to do would be to stop STOP. This particular book, for instance, describes an especially unhappy time in the dreadful lives of Violet, Klaus and Sunny Baudelaire, and if you have any sense at all you will shut this book immediately, drag it up a tall mountain and throw it off the very top STOP. There is no earthly reason why you should read even one more word about the misfortune, treachery and woe that are in store for the three Baudelaire children, any more than you should run into the street and throw yourself under the wheels of a bus STOP. This 'stop'-ended sentence is your very last chance to pretend the 'STOP' warning is a stop sign, and to stop the flood of despair that awaits you in this book, the heart-stopping horror that begins in the very next sentence, by obeying the 'STOP' and stopping STOP.

The Baudelaire orphans stopped. It was early in the morning, and the three children had been walking for hours across the flat and unfamiliar landscape. They were thirsty, lost, and exhausted, which are three good reasons to end a long walk, but they were also frightened, desperate, and not far from people who wanted to hurt them, which are three good reasons to continue. The siblings had abandoned all conversation hours ago, saving every last bit of their energy to put one foot in front of the other, but now they knew they had to stop, if only for a moment, and talk about what to do next.

The children were standing in front of the Last Chance General Store—the only building they had encountered since they began their long and frantic night-time walk. The outside of the store was covered with faded posters advertising what was sold, and by the eerie light of the half-moon, the Baudelaires could see that fresh limes, plastic knives, canned meat, white envelopes, mango-flavored candy, red wine, leather wallets, fashion magazines, goldfish bowls, sleeping bags, roasted figs, cardboard boxes, controversial vitamins, and many other things were available inside the store. Nowhere on the building, however, was there a poster advertising help, which is really what the Baudelaires needed.

'I think we should go inside,' said Violet, taking a ribbon out of her pocket to tie up her hair. Violet, the eldest Baudelaire, was probably the finest fourteen-year-old inventor in the world, and she always tied her hair up

3

in a ribbon when she had to solve a problem, and right now she was trying to invent a solution for the biggest problem she and her siblings had ever faced. 'Perhaps there's somebody in there who can help us in some way.'

'But perhaps there's somebody in there who has seen our pictures in the newspaper,' said Klaus, the middle Baudelaire, who had recently spent his thirteenth birthday in a filthy jail cell. Klaus had a real knack for remembering nearly every word of nearly all of the thousands of books he had read, and he frowned as he re-membered something untrue he had recently read about himself in the newspaper. 'If they read *The Daily Punctilio*,' he continued, 'perhaps they believe all those terrible things about us. Then they won't help us at all.'

'Agery!' Sunny said. Sunny was a baby, and as with most babies, different parts of her were growing at different rates. She had only four teeth, for example, but each of them was as sharp as that of an adult lion, and although she had recently learned to walk,

Sunny was still getting the hang of speaking in a way that all adults could understand. Her siblings, however, knew at once that she meant 'Well, we can't keep on walking forever,' and the two older Baudelaires nodded in agreement.

'Sunny's right,' Violet said. 'It's called the Last Chance General Store. That sounds like it's the only building for miles and miles. It might be our only opportunity to get some help.'

'And look,' Klaus said, pointing to a poster taped in a high corner of the building. 'We can send a telegram inside. Maybe we can get some help that way.'

'Who would we send a telegram to?' Violet asked, and once again the Baudelaires had to stop and think. If you are like most people, you have an assortment of friends and family you can call upon in times of trouble. For instance, if you woke up in the middle of the night and saw a masked woman trying to crawl through your bedroom window, you might call your mother or father to help you push her back out. If you found yourself hopelessly lost in the middle of a strange city, you might ask the police to give you a ride home. And if you were an author locked in an Italian restaurant that was slowly filling up with water, you might call upon your acquaintances in the locksmith, pasta, and sponge businesses to come and rescue you. But the Baudelaire children's trouble had begun with the news that their parents had been killed in a terrible fire, so they could not call upon their mother or father. The siblings could not call upon the police for assistance, because the police were among the people who had been chasing them all night long. And they could not call upon their acquaintances, because so many of the children's acquaintances were unable to help them. After the death of the Baudelaire parents, Violet, Klaus, and Sunny had found themselves under the care of a variety of guardians. Some of them had been cruel. Some of them had been murdered. And one of them had been Count Olaf, a greedy and treacherous villain who was the real reason they were all by themselves in the middle of the night, standing in front of the Last Chance General Store, wondering who in the world they could call upon for help.

'Poe,' Sunny said finally. She was talking about Mr. Poe, a banker with a nasty cough, who was in charge of taking care of the children following their parents' death. Mr. Poe had never been particularly helpful, but he was not cruel, murdered, or Count Olaf, and those seemed to be reasons enough to contact him.

'I guess we could try Mr. Poe,' Klaus agreed. 'The worst he could do would be to say no.'

'Or cough,' Violet said with a small smile. Her siblings smiled hack, and the three children pushed open the rusty door and walked inside.

'Lou, is that you?' called out a voice, but the children could not see who it belonged to. The inside of the Last Chance General Store was as crowded as its outside, with every inch of space crammed full of things for sale. There were shelves of canned asparagus and racks of fountain pens, next to barrels of onions and crates full of peacock feathers. There were cooking utensils nailed to the walls and chandeliers hanging from the ceiling, and the floor was made out of thousands of different kinds of tiles, each one stamped with a price tag. 'Are you delivering the morning paper?' the voice asked.

'No,' Violet replied, as the Baudelaires tried to make their way toward the person who was talking. With difficulty they stepped over a carton of cat food and rounded a corner, only to find rows and rows of fishnets blocking their way.

'I'm not surprised, Lou,' the voice continued, as the siblings doubled back past a stack of mirrors and a pile of socks and headed down an aisle filled with pots of ivy and books of matches. 'I usually don't expect *The Daily Punctilio* until after the Volunteers Fighting Disease arrive.'

The children stopped looking for the source of the voice for a moment, and looked at one another, thinking of their friends Duncan and Isadora

Quagmire. Duncan and Isadora were two triplets who, like the Baudelaires, had lost their parents, along with their brother, Quigley, in a terrible fire. The Quagmires had fallen into Olaf's hands a couple of times and had only recently escaped, but the Baudelaires did not know if they would see their friends ever again or learn a secret that the triplets had discovered and written down in their notebooks. The secret concerned the initials V.F.D., but the only other clues that the Baudelaires had were a few pages from Duncan's and Isadora's notebooks, and the three siblings had scarcely found the time to look them over. Could Volunteers Fighting Disease finally be the answer the children were searching for?

'No, we're not Lou,' Violet called out. 'We're three children, and we need to send a telegram.'

'A telegram?' called the voice, and as the children rounded another corner they almost ran right into the man who was talking to them. He was very short, shorter than both Violet and Klaus, and looked like he hadn't slept or shaved in quite a long time. He was wearing two different shoes, each with a price tag, and several shirts and hats at once. He was so covered in merchandise that he almost looked like part of the store, except for his friendly smile and dirty fingernails.

'You're certainly not Lou,' he said. 'Lou is one chubby man, and you are three skinny children. What are you doing around here so early? It's dangerous around here, you know. I've heard that this morning's *Daily Punctilio* has a story about three murderers who are lurking around this very neighborhood, but I haven't read it yet.'

'Newspaper stories aren't always accurate,' Klaus said nervously.

The shopkeeper frowned. 'Nonsense,' he said. '*The Daily Punctilio* wouldn't print things that aren't true. If the newspaper says somebody is a murderer, then they are a murderer and that's the end of it. Now, you say you wanted to send a telegram?'

'Yes,' Violet said. 'To Mr. Poe at

Mulctuary Money Management, in the city.'

'It will cost quite a bit of money to send a telegram all the way to the city,' the shopkeeper said, and the Baudelaires looked at one another in dismay.

'We don't have any money with us,' Klaus admitted. 'We're three orphans, and the only money we have is being looked after by Mr. Poe. Please, sir.'

'Sos!' Sunny said.

'My sister means "It's an emergency situation",' Violet explained, 'and it is.'

The shopkeeper looked at them for a moment, and then shrugged. 'If it's really an emergency situation,' he said, 'then I won't charge you. I never charge anything for things if they're really important. Volunteers Fighting Disease, for instance. Whenever they stop by, I give them gasoline for free because they do such wonderful work.'

'What exactly do they do?' Violet asked.

'They fight disease, of course,' the shopkeeper replied. 'V.F.D. stop by here early each morning on their way

11

to the hospital. Every day they devote themselves to cheering up patients, and I don't have the heart to charge them for anything.'

'You're a very kind man,' Klaus replied.

'Well, it's very kind of you to say so,' the shopkeeper replied. 'Now, the device for sending telegrams is over there, next to all those porcelain kittens. I'll help you.'

'We can do it ourselves,' Violet said. 'I built one of those devices myself when I was seven, so I know how to connect the electronic circuit.'

'And I've read two books about Morse code,' Klaus said. 'So I can translate our message into electronic signals.'

'Help!' Sunny said.

'What a talented group of children,' the shopkeeper said with a smile. 'Well, I'll leave you three alone. I hope that this Mr. Poe person can help you with your emergency situation.'

'Thank you very much, sir,' Violet said. 'I hope so, too.'

The shopkeeper gave the children a

little wave and disappeared behind a display of potato peelers, and the Baudelaires looked at one another in excitement.

'Volunteers Fighting Disease?' Klaus whispered to Violet. 'Do you think we've finally found the real meaning of V.F.D.?'

'Jacques!' Sunny said.

'Jacques did say something about working as a volunteer,' Klaus agreed. 'If only we had a few moments to look over the pages from the Quagmire notebooks. They're still in my pocket.'

'First things first,' Violet said. 'Let's send the telegram to Mr. Poe. If Lou delivers this morning's *Daily Punctilio*, the shopkeeper is going to stop thinking we're a group of talented children and start thinking we're murderers.'

'You're right,' Klaus said. 'After Mr. Poe gets us out of this mess, we'll have time to think about these other things.'

'Trosslik,' Sunny said. She meant something along the lines of, 'You mean *if* Mr. Poe gets us out of this mess,' and her siblings nodded grimly

13

and went over to take a look at the telegram device. It was an arrangement of dials, wires, and strange metal implements that I would have been too scared to even touch, but the Baudelaires approached it with confidence.

'I'm pretty sure we can operate this,' Violet said. 'It looks fairly simple. See, Klaus, you use these two metal strips to tap out the message in Morse code, and I will connect the circuit over here. Sunny, you stand here and put on these earphones to make sure you can hear the signal being transmitted. Let's step to it.'

The children stepped to it, a phrase which here means 'took their positions around the telegram device.' Violet turned a dial, Sunny put on her earphones, and Klaus wiped the lenses of his glasses so he could be sure to see what he was doing. The siblings nodded at one another, and Klaus began to speak out loud as he tapped out the message in code.

'To: Mr. Poe at Mulctuary Money Management,' Klaus said. 'From:

Violet, Klaus, and Sunny Baudelaire. Please do not believe the story about us printed in *The Daily Punctilio* STOP. Count Olaf is not really dead, and we did not really murder him STOP'

'Arrete?' Sunny asked.

' "STOP" is the code for the end of a sentence,' Klaus explained. 'Now, what should I say next?'

'Soon after our arrival in the town of V.F.D. we were informed that Count Olaf had been captured STOP,' Violet dictated. 'Although the arrested man had an eye tattooed on his ankle and one eyebrow instead of two, he was not Count Olaf STOP. His name was Jacques Snicket STOP'

'The next day he was found murdered, and Count Olaf arrived in town along with his girlfriend, Esmé Squalor STOP,' Klaus continued, tapping away. 'As part of his plan to steal the fortune our parents left behind, Count Olaf disguised himself as a detective and convinced the town of V.F.D. that we were the murderers STOP'

'Uckner,' Sunny suggested, and

Klaus translated what she said into English, and then into Morse code: 'Meanwhile we discovered where the Quagmire triplets were being hidden, and helped them escape STOP. The Quagmires managed to give us a few scraps of their note-books so we could try to learn the real meaning of V.F.D. STOP'

'We have managed to flee from the citizens of the town, who want to burn us at the stake for a murder that we did not commit STOP,' Violet said, and Klaus quickly tapped the sentence out into code before adding two last sentences of his own.

'Please reply at once STOP. We are in grave danger STOP.'

Klaus tapped out the last P in 'STOP' and then looked at his sisters. 'We are in grave danger,' he said again, although his hand did not move on the device.

'You already sent that sentence,' Violet said.

'I know,' Klaus said quietly. 'I wasn't putting it into the telegram again. I was just saying it. We are in grave danger.

It's almost as if I didn't realize how grave the danger was until I tapped it out into a telegram.'

'Ilimi,' Sunny said, and took off her earphones so she could lay her head on Klaus's shoulder.

'I'm scared, too,' Violet admitted, patting her sister's shoulder. 'But I'm sure Mr. Poe will help us. We can't be expected to solve this problem all by ourselves.'

'But that's how we've solved every other problem,' Klaus said, 'ever since the fire. Mr. Poe has never done anything except send us to one disastrous home after another.'

'He'll help us this time,' Violet insisted, although she did not sound very sure. 'Just watch the device. He'll send back a telegram any moment now.'

'But what if he doesn't?' Klaus asked.

'Chonex,' Sunny murmured, and wriggled closer to her siblings. She meant something along the lines of 'Then we're all alone,' which is a curious thing to say when you are with

17

your two siblings, in the middle of a store so stuffed with merchandise you can hardly move. But as they sat closely together, looking at the telegram device, it did not seem curious to the Baudelaires. They were surrounded by nylon rope, floor wax, soup bowls, window curtains, wooden rocking horses, top hats, fiber-optic cable, pink lipstick, dried apricots, magnifying glasses, black umbrellas, slender paintbrushes, French horns, and each other, but as the Baudelaire orphans sat and waited for a reply to their telegram, they only felt more and more alone.

CHAPTER TWO

Of all the ridiculous expressions people use—and people use a great many ridiculous expressions—one of the most ridiculous is 'No news is good news.' 'No news is good news' simply means that if you don't hear from someone, everything is probably fine, and you can see at once why this expression makes such little sense, because everything being fine is only one of many, many reasons why someone may not contact you. Perhaps they are tied up. Maybe they are surrounded by fierce weasels, or perhaps they are wedged tightly between two refrigerators and cannot get themselves out. The expression might well be changed to 'No news is bad news,' except that people may not be able to contact you because they have just been crowned king or are competing in a gymnastics tournament. The point is that there is no way to know why someone has not contacted you, until they contact you and explain themselves. For this reason, the sensible expression would be 'No news is no news,' except that it is so obvious it is hardly an expression at all.

Obvious or not, however, it is the proper way to describe what happened to the Baudelaires after they sent the desperate telegram to Mr. Poe. Violet, Klaus, and Sunny sat and stared at the telegram device for hours, waiting for some sign of the banker's reply. As the hour grew later and later, they took turns dozing against the merchandise of the Last Chance General Store, hoping for any response from the man who was in charge of the orphans' affairs. And as the first few rays of dawn shone through the window, illuminating all of the price tags in the store, the only news the children had received was that the shopkeeper had made some fresh cranberry muffins.

'I've made some fresh cranberry

muffins,' the shopkeeper said, peeking around a tower of flour sifters. He was wearing at least two pot holders on each hand and was carrying the muffins on a stack of different-colored trays. 'Normally I would put them up for sale, between the phonograph records and the garden rakes, but I hate to think of you three children going without breakfast when there are vicious murderers on the loose, so have some for yourself, free of charge.'

'That's very kind of you,' Violet said, as she and her siblings each took a muffin from the shopkeeper's top tray. The Baudelaires, who had not eaten since they left the village, soon made short work—a phrase which here means 'ate every warm, sweet crumb'—of the pastries.

'Goodness, you're hungry,' the shopkeeper said. 'Did everything go all right with the telegram? Have you received a reply?'

'Not yet,' Klaus said.

'Well, don't worry your tiny heads about it,' the shopkeeper replied. 'Remember, no news is good news.'

'No news is good news?' called out a voice from somewhere in the store. 'I have some news for you, Milt. All about those murderers.'

'Lou!' the shopkeeper called in delight, and then turned to the children. 'Excuse me, please,' he said. 'Lou's here with *The Daily Punctilio*.'

The shopkeeper walked through a bunch of rugs hanging from the ceiling, and the Baudelaires looked at one another in dismay.

'What'll we do?' Klaus whispered to his sisters. 'If the newspaper has arrived, the shopkeeper will read that we're murderers. We'd better run away.'

'But if we run away,' Violet said, 'Mr. Poe won't be able to contact us.'

'Gykree!' Sunny cried, which meant 'He's had all night to contact us, and we haven't heard from him.'

'Lou?' they heard the shopkeeper call out. 'Where are you, Lou?'

'I'm over by the pepper grinders,' the delivery-person called out in return. 'And wait till you read this story about the three murderers of that Count. It's

22

got pictures and everything. I saw the police on the way here, and they said they were closing in. The only people they allowed in the area were me and those volunteer people. They're going to capture those kids and send them right to jail.'

'Kids?' the shopkeeper said. 'The murderers are kids?'

'Yep,' the delivery-person replied. 'See for yourself.'

The children looked at one another, and Sunny gave a little whimper of fear. Across the store they could hear the rustling of paper and then the excited voice of the shopkeeper.

'I know those kids!' he cried. 'They're in my store right now! I just gave them some muffins!'

'You gave muffins to murderers?' Lou said. 'That's not right, Milt. Criminals should be punished, not fed pastries.'

'I didn't know they were murderers then,' the shopkeeper explained, 'but I sure know now. It says so right here in *The Daily Punctilio.* Call the police, Lou! I'll grab these murderers and make sure they don't escape.'

The Baudelaires wasted no more time, and began to run in the opposite direction from the men's voices, down an aisle of safety pins and candy canes. 'Let's head toward those ceramic ashtrays,' Violet whispered. 'I think we can exit that way.'

'But what happens when we exit?' Klaus whispered back. 'The delivery person said that the police were closing in.'

'Mulick!' Sunny cried, which meant 'Let's discuss that at a later time!'

'Egad!' The children could hear the shopkeeper's surprised voice from several aisles over. 'Lou, the kids aren't here! Keep an eye out for them.'

'What do they look like?' the delivery-person called back.

'They look like three innocent children,' the shopkeeper said, 'but they're really vicious criminals. Be careful.'

The children ran around a corner and ducked into the next aisle, pressing themselves against a rack of construction paper and canned peas as

24

they listened to the hurrying footsteps of the delivery-person. 'Wherever you murderers are,' he called, 'you'd better give up!'

'We're not murderers!' Violet cried in frustration.

'Of course you're murderers!' the shopkeeper answered. 'It says so in the newspaper!'

'Plus,' the delivery-person said in a sneering voice, 'if you're not murderers, why are you hiding and running?'

Violet started to answer, but Klaus covered her mouth before she could say anything more. 'They'll be able to tell where we are by our voices,' he whispered. 'Just let them talk, and maybe we can escape.'

'Lou, do you see them?' called the shopkeeper.

'No, but they can't hide forever,' the delivery-person said. 'I'm going to look over by the undershirts!'

The Baudelaires looked ahead of them and saw a pile of white undershirts that happened to be on sale. Gasping, the children doubled back, and ran down an aisle covered in ticking clocks.

'I'm going to try the clock aisle!' the shopkeeper cried. 'They can't hide forever!'

The children hurried down the aisle, sprinted past a rack of towel racks and piggy banks, and scurried around a display of sensible plaid skirts. Finally, over the top shelf of an aisle containing nothing but different kinds of bedroom slippers, Violet spotted a glimpse of the exit, and silently pointed the way to her siblings.

'I bet they're in the sausage aisle!' the shopkeeper said.

'I bet they're near the bathtub display!' the delivery-person called.

'They can't hide forever!' the shopkeeper cried.

The Baudelaires took a deep breath, and then bolted toward the exit of the Last Chance General Store, but as soon as they got outside they realized the shopkeeper was right. The sun was rising, revealing the flat and desolate landscape the children had walked across all night. In a few hours the entire countryside would be covered in sunlight, and the land was so flat that the children would be seen from far, far away. They couldn't hide forever, and as Violet, Klaus, and Sunny stood outside the Last Chance General Store, it seemed that they couldn't hide for even one more instant.

'Look!' Klaus said, and pointed in the direction of the rising sun. Parked a ways from the store was a square, gray van with the letters V.F.D. printed on its side.

'That must be the Volunteers Fighting Disease,' Violet said. 'The delivery-person said only he and the volunteers were allowed in the area.'

'Then they're the only way we can hide,' Klaus said. 'If we can sneak aboard that van, we can escape from the police, at least for now.'

'But this might be the right V.F.D.,' Violet said. 'If these volunteers are part of the sinister secret the Quagmire triplets tried to tell us about, we might be going from a bad situation to a worse one.'

'Or,' Klaus said, 'it might get us

closer to solving the mystery of Jacques Snicket. Remember, he said he worked as a volunteer, right before he was murdered.'

'It won't do us any good to solve the mystery of Jacques Snicket,' Violet said, 'if we're in jail.'

'Blusin,' Sunny said. She meant something along the lines of, 'We don't have much choice,' and in small, tottering steps she led her siblings toward the V.F.D. van.

'But how will we get on the van?' Violet asked, walking alongside her sister.

'What will we say to the volunteers?' Klaus asked, hurrying to catch up.

'Impro,' Sunny said, which meant 'We'll think of something,' but for once the three children didn't have to think of something. As the youngsters reached the van, a friendly-looking man with a guitar in his hands and a beard on his face leaned out of one of the windows and called to them.

'We almost left you behind, brother and sisters!' he said. 'We filled the van up with free gas, and now we're all set to head off to the hospital.' With a smile, the man unlatched the door of the van and opened it, beckoning to the three children. 'Climb aboard,' he said. 'We don't want our volunteers to get lost before we even sing the first verse. I heard something about murderers lurking around this area.'

'Did you read it in the newspaper?' Klaus asked nervously.

The bearded man laughed, and strummed a cheerful chord on his guitar. 'Oh, no,' he said. 'We don't read the newspaper. It's too depressing. Our motto is "No news is good news." You must be new volunteers, not to know that. Well, hop in.'

The Baudelaires hesitated. As I'm sure you know, it is rarely a good idea to get into an automobile with somebody you haven't met before, particularly if the person believes in such nonsense as 'No news is good news.' But it is *never* a good idea to stand around a flat and empty landscape while the police are closing in to arrest you for a crime you have not committed, and the three children paused for a moment to decide between doing something which is rarely a good idea, and something that is never a good idea. They looked at the bearded man with the guitar. They looked at each other. And then they looked back at the Last Chance General Store, where they saw the shopkeeper, rushing out of the front door and toward the van.

'O.K.,' Violet said finally. 'We'll hop in.'

The bearded man smiled, and the children stepped into the V.F.D. van and shut the door behind them. They did not hop, even though the man had asked them to 'hop in,' because hopping is something done in the cheerful moments of one's life. A plumber might hop, for instance, if she finally fixed a particularly difficult leak in someone's shower. A sculptor would hop if his sculpture of four basset hounds playing cards was finally finished. And I would hop like nobody has ever hopped before, if I could somehow go back to that terrible Thursday, and stop Beatrice from attending that afternoon tea where she met Esmé Squalor for the first time.

But Violet, Klaus, and Sunny did not hop, because they were not plumbers fixing leaks, or sculptors finishing works of art, or authors magically erasing a series of unfortunate events. They were three desperate children, falsely accused of murder, forced to run out of a store into a stranger's automobile to avoid capture by the police. The Baudelaires were not hopping, even as the van started its engine and began to drive away from the Last Chance General Store, ignoring the desperate signals of the shopkeeper as he ran to try to stop them. As the V.F.D. van began to drive across the lonely landscape, the Baudelaire orphans were not sure they would ever hop again.

CHAPTER THREE

We are Volunteers Fighting Disease,
And we're cheerful all day long.
If someone said that we were sad,
That person would be wrong.

We visit people who are sick,
And try to make them smile,
Even if their noses bleed,
Or if they cough up bile.

Tra la la, Fiddle dee dee,
Hope you get well soon.
Ho ho ho, hee hee hee,
Have a heart-shaped balloon.

We visit people who are ill,
And try to make them laugh,
Even when the doctor says
He must saw them in half.

We sing and sing all night and day,
And then we sing some more.
We sing to boys with broken bones
And girls whose throats are sore.

Tra la la, Fiddle dee dee,
Hope you get well soon.
Ho ho ho, hee hee hee,
Have a heart-shaped balloon.

We sing to men with measles,
And to women with the flu,

33

And if you breathe in deadly germs,
We'll probably sing to you.

Tra la la, Fiddle dee dee,
Hope you get well soon.
Ho ho ho, hee hee hee,
Have a heart-shaped balloon.

An associate of mine named William Congreve once wrote a very sad play that begins with the line 'Music has charms to soothe a savage breast,' a sentence which here means that if you are nervous or upset, you might listen to some music to calm you down or cheer you up. For instance, as I crouch here behind the altar of the Cathedral of the Alleged Virgin, a friend of mine is playing a sonata on the pipe organ, to calm me down and so the sounds of my typewriter will not be heard by the worshippers sitting in the pews. The mournful melody of the sonata reminds me of a tune my father used to sing when he did the dishes, and as I listen to it I can temporarily forget six or seven of my troubles.

But the soothing effect of music on a

savage breast obviously depends on what kind of music is being played, and I'm sorry to say that as the Baudelaire orphans listened to the song of V.F.D., they did not feel even one bit less nervous or upset. When Violet, Klaus, and Sunny first boarded the V.F.D. van, they were so worried about avoiding capture that they scarcely took a look around them until they were quite far away from the Last Chance General Store. But when the shopkeeper was merely a speck on the flat and empty landscape, the children turned their attention to their new hiding place. There were about twenty people in the van, and every single one of them was exceedingly cheerful. There were cheerful men, cheerful women, a handful of cheerful children, and a very cheerful driver who occasionally took his eyes off the road to grin cheerfully at all his passengers. When the Baudelaires took a long trip in an automobile, they liked to pass the time reading or looking at the scenery and thinking their own private thoughts, but as soon as the van pulled away from the general store, the bearded man began playing his guitar and led all of the Volunteers Fighting Disease in a cheerful song, and each 'tra la la' only made the Baudelaires more anxious than before. When the volunteers began to sing the verse about people's noses bleeding, the siblings were sure someone would stop singing and say, 'Wait a minute! These three children weren't on the van before! They don't belong here!' When the singers reached the verse about the doctor sawing someone in half, the children were certain someone would stop singing and say, 'Wait a minute! Those three people don't know the lyrics to the song! They don't belong here!' And when the cheerful passengers sung the section of the song discussing deadly germs, the siblings were unequivocally positive that someone would stop singing and say, 'Wait a minute! Those three children are the murderers described in *The Daily Punctilio!* They don't belong here!'

But the Volunteers Fighting Disease

were too cheerful to wait a minute. They believed so strongly that no news is good news that none of them had even glanced at *The Daily Punctilio.* And they were too busy singing to notice that the Baudelaires didn't belong on the van.

'Boy, do I love that song!' the bearded man said, when the last chorus had ended. 'I could sing it all the way to Heimlich Hospital. But I guess we'd better save our voices for the day's work. So why don't we settle down and have cheerful conversations until we arrive?'

'That sounds super-duper!' said one of the volunteers, and everyone nodded in agreement. The bearded man put away his guitar and sat down next to the Baudelaires.

'We'd better make up false names,' Violet whispered to Klaus, 'so no one will learn who we are.'

'But *The Daily Punctilio* got our names wrong,' Klaus whispered back, 'so maybe we should use our real names.'

'Well, let's get to know each other,'

the bearded man said cheerfully. 'I like to get to know each and every one of our volunteers.'

'Well, my name is Sally,' Violet began, 'and—'

'No, no,' the bearded man said. 'We don't use names in V.F.D. We just call everybody "sister" and "brother," because we believe all people are sisters and brothers.'

'I'm confused,' Klaus said. 'I always thought that brothers and sisters are people who share the same parents.'

'Not always, brother,' the bearded man said. 'Sometimes brothers and sisters are just people who are united for a common cause.'

'Does that mean, brother,' Violet said, trying this new use of the word 'brother' and not liking it much, 'that you don't know the names of anyone in this van?'

'That's right, sister,' the bearded man said.

'And so you've never known the name of anyone who's been a Volunteer Fighting Disease?' Klaus asked.

'Not a single one,' the bearded man said. 'Why do you ask?'

'There's a person we know,' Violet said carefully, 'who we think might have been in V.F.D. He had one eyebrow instead of two, and a tattoo of an eye on his ankle.'

The bearded man frowned. 'I don't know anyone of that description,' he said, 'and I've been with the Volunteers Fighting Disease since the organization first started.'

'Rats!' Sunny said.

'What my sister means,' Klaus said, 'is that we're disappointed. We were hoping to learn more about this person.'

'Are you sure he was in Volunteers Fighting Disease?' the bearded man asked.

'No,' Klaus admitted. 'We just know he worked in the volunteer something.'

'Well, there are lots of volunteer somethings,' the bearded man replied. 'What you kids need is some sort of Library of Records.'

'A Library of Records?' Violet said.

'A Library of Records is a place

where official information is stored,' the bearded man said. 'In a Library of Records, you could find a list of every single volunteer organization in the world. Or you could look up this person and see if there's a file on him. Perhaps that would tell you where he worked.'

'Or how he knew our parents,' Klaus said, speaking out loud without thinking.

'Your parents?' the bearded man said, looking around the van. 'Are they here, too?'

The Baudelaires looked at one another, wishing that their parents were there on the van, even though it would be awkward to call their father 'brother' and their mother 'sister.' Sometimes it seemed to the children that it had been hundreds and hundreds of years since that terrible day at the beach when Mr. Poe brought them the dreadful news, but just as often it seemed as if it had been only minutes. Violet could picture her father, sitting next to her, perhaps pointing out something interesting he had seen through the window. Klaus could picture his mother, smiling and shaking her head in amusement at the ridiculous lyrics of the V.F.D. song. And Sunny could picture all five Baudelaires, together again, with nobody fleeing from the police, or accused of murder, or trying desperately to solve mysteries, or worst of all, gone forever in a terrible fire. But just because you can picture something does not make it so. The Baudelaire parents were not in the van, and the children looked at the bearded man and shook their heads sadly.

'My, you look glum,' the bearded man said. 'Well, don't worry. I'm sure wherever your parents are, they're having a good time, so let's not see any frowny faces. Being cheerful is the whole point of Volunteers Fighting Disease.'

'What exactly will we be doing at the hospital?' Violet asked, eager to change the subject.

'Just what V.F.D. says,' the bearded man replied. 'We're volunteers, and we'll be fighting diseases.'

'I hope we won't be giving shots,' Klaus said. 'Needles make me a bit nervous.'

'Of course we won't be giving shots,' the bearded man said. 'We only do cheerful things. Mostly we wander the halls singing to sick people, and giving them heart-shaped balloons, like the song says.'

'But how does that fight disease?' Violet said.

'Because getting a cheerful balloon helps people picture getting better, and if you picture something, it makes it so,' the bearded man explained. 'After all, a cheerful attitude is the most effective tool against sickness.'

'I thought antibiotics were,' Klaus said. 'Echinacea!'

Sunny said. She meant 'Or well-tested herbal remedies,' but the bearded man had stopped paying attention to the children and was looking out the window.

'We've arrived, volunteers!' he called out. 'We're at Heimlich Hospital!' He turned to the Baudelaires and pointed out at the horizon. 'Isn't it a beautiful building?'

The children looked out the windows of the van and found that they could only half agree with the bearded man, for the simple reason that Heimlich Hospital was only half a building, or at best two thirds. The left side of the hospital was a shiny white structure, with a row of tall pillars and small carved portraits of famous doctors over each window. In front of the building was a neatly mowed lawn, with occasional patches of brightly colored wildflowers. But the right side of the hospital was scarcely a structure at all, let alone a beautiful one. There were a few boards nailed together into rectangles, and a few planks nailed down for floors, but there were no walls or windows, so it looked like a drawing of a hospital rather than a hospital itself. There was no sign of any pillars and not even one carved doctor portrait on this half-finished side, just a few sheets of plastic fluttering in the wind, and instead of a lawn there was just an empty field of dirt. It was as if the architect in charge of constructing the building had decided halfway through that he'd rather go on a picnic, and had never returned. The driver parked the van underneath a sign that was half finished, too: the word 'Heimlich' was in fancy gold letters on a clean white square of wood, but the word 'Hospital' was scrawled in ballpoint pen on a piece of cardboard ripped from an old box.

'I'm sure they'll finish it someday,' the bearded man continued. 'But in the meantime, we can picture the other half, and picturing something makes it so. Now, let's picture ourselves getting out of the van.'

The three Baudelaires did not have to picture it, but they followed the bearded man and the rest of the volunteers out of the van and onto the lawn in front of the prettier half of the hospital. The members of V.F.D. were stretching their arms and legs after the long drive, and helping the bearded man remove a big bunch of heart-shaped balloons from the back of the van, but the children merely stood around anxiously and tried to figure

44

out what to do next.

'Where should we go?' Violet asked. 'If we walk around the hallways of the hospital singing to people, someone will recognize us.'

'That's true,' Klaus said. 'The doctors, nurses, administrators, and patients can't all believe that no news is good news. I'm sure some of them have read this morning's *Daily Punctilio*.'

'Aronec,' Sunny said, which meant 'And we're not getting any closer to learning anything about V.F.D., or Jacques Snicket.'

'That's true,' Violet agreed. 'Maybe we need to find a Library of Records, like the bearded man said.'

'But where can we find one?' Klaus asked. 'We're in the middle of nowhere.'

'No walk!' Sunny said.

'I don't want to start all that walking again either,' Violet said, 'but I don't see what else we can do.'

'O.K., volunteers!' the bearded man said. He took his guitar out of the van and began playing some cheerful and familiar chords. 'Everyone take a heart-shaped balloon and start singing!

'We are Volunteers Fighting Disease,
And we're cheerful all day long,
If someone said that we were sad,
That person would be—'

'Attention!' interrupted a voice that seemed to come from the sky. The voice was female but very scratchy and faint, as if the voice were that of a woman talking with a piece of aluminum foil over her mouth. 'Your attention please!'

'Shh, everybody!' the bearded man said, stopping the song. 'That's Babs, the Head of Human Resources at the hospital. She must have an important announcement.'

'Attention!' the voice said. 'This is Babs, Head of Human Resources. I have an important announcement.'

'Where is she?' Klaus asked him, worried that she might recognize the three accused murderers hiding in V.F.D.

'In the hospital someplace,' the bearded man replied. 'She prefers

46

communicating over the intercom.'

The word 'intercom' here refers to someone talking into a microphone someplace and having their voice come out of speakers someplace else, and sure enough the children noticed a small row of square speakers placed on the finished half of the building, just above the doctor portraits. 'Attention!' the voice said again, and it became even scratchier and fainter, as if the woman with the piece of aluminum foil over her mouth had fallen into a swimming pool filled with fizzy soda. This is not a pleasant way to hear someone talk, and yet as soon as Babs made her announcement, the savage breasts of the Baudelaire orphans were instantly soothed, as if the scratchy and faint voice were a calming piece of music. But the Baudelaires did not feel better because of the way Babs's voice sounded. The announcement soothed the children's savage breasts because of what it said.

'I need three members of the Volunteers Fighting Disease who are willing to be given a new assignment,' said the voice. 'Those three volunteers should report immediately to my office, which is the seventeenth door on the left as you enter the finished half of the building. Instead of walking around the hallways of the hospital singing to people, these three volunteers will be working in the Library of Records here at Heimlich Hospital.'

CHAPTER FOUR

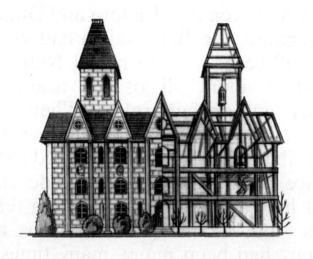

Whether you have been sent to see the principal of your school for throwing wet paper towels at the ceiling to see if they stick, or taken to the dentist to plead with him to hollow out one of your teeth so you can smuggle a single page of your latest book past the guards at the airport, it is never a pleasant feeling to stand outside the door of an office, and as the Baudelaire orphans stood at the door reading 'Office of the Head of Human Resources' they were reminded of all the unpleasant offices they had recently visited. On their very first day at Prufrock Preparatory School, before they had even met Isadora and Duncan Quagmire, the Baudelaires had visited the office of Vice Principal Nero and learned about all of the academy's strict and unfair rules. When they worked at Lucky Smells Lumber-mill, the siblings had been summoned to the office of the owner, who made clear just how dreadful their situation really was. And, of course, Violet, Klaus, and Sunny had been many, many times to Mr. Poe's office at the bank, where he coughed and talked on the phone and made decisions about the Baudelaires' future that had not proved to be good ones. But even if the children had not had all these unfortunate experiences in offices, it was perfectly understandable that the Baudelaire children had to stand for a few moments in front of the seventeenth door on the left, and gather their courage to knock.

'I'm not sure we should take this risk,' Violet said. 'If Babs has read this morning's edition of *The Daily Punctilio*, she'll recognize us as soon as we walk through the door. We might as well be knocking on the door of our jail cell.'

'But the Library of Records might be our only hope,' Klaus said. 'We need to find out who Jacques Snicket really was—where he worked, and how he knew us. If we get some evidence, we can convince people that Count Olaf is still alive and that we're not murderers.'

'Curoy,' Sunny added, which meant 'Besides, the Quagmire triplets are far, far away, and we have only a few pages of their notebooks. We need to find the real meaning of V.F.D.'

'Sunny's right,' Klaus said. 'In the Library of Records, we might even solve the mystery of that underground passageway that led from Jerome and Esmé Squalor's apartment to the ashy remains of the Baudelaire mansion.'

'Afficu,' Sunny said. She meant something like 'And the only way we'll get into the Library of Records is if we talk to Babs, so it's a risk we have to take.'

'All right,' Violet said, looking down at her sister and smiling. 'You've convinced me. But if Babs begins looking at us suspiciously, we'll leave, agreed?'

'Agreed,' Klaus said.

'Yep,' Sunny said, and knocked on the door.

'Who is it?' Babs's voice called out.

'It's three members of Volunteers Fighting Disease,' Violet replied. 'We're here to volunteer at the Library of Records.'

'Come in,' Babs commanded, and the children opened the door and walked into the office. 'I was wondering when someone would show up,' the Head of Human Resources continued. 'I was just finishing up reading this morning's paper. These three terrible children are running around killing people.'

The Baudelaires looked at one another and were about to run back out the door when they saw something

52

in the office that changed their minds. The office of the Head of Human Resources at Heimlich Hospital was a small one, with a small desk, two small chairs, and a small window decorated with two small curtains. On the windowsill was a small vase of yellow flowers and on the wall was a small tasteful portrait of a man leading a horse to a small pond of fresh water. But it was not the furnishings, the flower arrangement, or the tasteful artwork that made the three orphans stop.

Babs's voice had come from the direction of the desk, which the Baudelaires had expected, but what they hadn't expected was that Babs was not sitting behind the desk, or on the desk or even beneath it. Instead, a small square intercom speaker—just like the ones on the outside of the hospital—had been placed in the middle of the desk, and it was from this speaker that the speaking had been spoken. It was strange to hear speaking from a speaker instead of from the person who was speaking, but the children realized they could not be recognized if Babs could not see them, so they did not run out of the room.

'We're three children, too,' Violet said to the speaker, trying to be as honest as she could, 'but we'd much rather volunteer in the hospital than embark on a life of crime.'

'If you're children, then be silent!' Babs's voice said rudely. 'In my opinion, children should be seen and not heard. I'm an adult, so it follows that I should be heard and not seen. That's why I work exclusively over the intercom. You will be working exclusively with the most important thing we do in this hospital. Can you guess what it is?'

'Healing sick people?' Klaus guessed.

'Be silent!' the speaker commanded. 'Children should be seen and not heard, remember? Just because I can't see you doesn't mean you should start babbling about sick people. You're wrong, anyway. The most important thing we do at the hospital is paperwork, and you will be working at the Library of Records, filing paperwork. I'm sure this will be difficult for you, because children never have any administrative experience.'

'Hend,' said Sunny in disagreement. Violet was about to explain that her sister meant something along the lines of 'Actually, I worked as an administrative assistant at Prufrock Preparatory School,' but the intercom speaker was too busy reproving the Baudelaires, a phrase which here means 'shouting "Be silent!"' at every opportunity.

'Be silent!' the speaker shouted. 'Instead of chattering away, report to the Library of Records at once. The Library of Records is located in the basement, at the very bottom of the staircase next to this office. You'll go straight there every morning when the van arrives at Heimlich Hospital, and you'll return straight to the van at the end of each day. The van will take you back home. Are there any questions?'

The Baudelaires had plenty of questions, of course, but they did not ask them. They knew that if they said even one word, the intercom speaker would command them to be silent, and besides, they were eager to get to the Library of Records, where they hoped to answer the most important questions of their lives.

'Excellent!' the speaker said. 'You're learning to be seen instead of heard. Now, get out of this office.'

The children got out of that office and quickly found the staircase the speaker had mentioned. The Baudelaires were glad that the route to the Library of Records was so easy to remember, because Heimlich Hospital seemed like a place where it would be very easy to get lost. The staircase curved this way and that, leading to many doors and corridors, and every ten feet or so, nailed to the wall just below an intercom speaker there was a complicated map of the hospital, filled with arrows, stars, and other symbols the Baudelaires did not recognize. Every so often, the children would see someone from the hospital walking toward them. Although neither the

Volunteers Fighting Disease nor the Head of Human Resources had recognized the three children, it was certain that someone in the hospital must have read *The Daily Punctilio*, and the Baudelaires did not want to be seen or heard, and they would have to turn and face the wall, pretending to consult the map so anyone walking by would not see their faces.

'That was close,' Violet sighed in relief, when a group of chatting doctors had gone by without even glancing at the youngsters.

'It was close,' Klaus agreed, 'and we don't want it to get any closer. I don't think we should get back on the van at the end of the day—or any other day. Sooner or later we're bound to be recognized.'

'You're right,' Violet said. 'We'd have to walk back through the hospital every day, just to get to the van. But where will we go at night? People will think it is odd if three children are sleeping in the Library of Records.'

'Half,' Sunny suggested.

'That's a pretty good idea,' Violet

replied. 'We could sleep in the unfinished half of the hospital. Nobody will go there at night.'

'Sleep all by ourselves, in a half-finished room?' Klaus asked. 'It'll be cold and dark.'

'It can't be much worse than the Orphans Shack at Prufrock Prep,' Violet said.

'Danya,' Sunny said, which meant 'Or the bedroom at Count Olaf's house.'

Klaus shuddered, remembering how terrible it was when Count Olaf had been their guardian. 'You're right,' he said, stopping at a door which read 'Library of Records.'

'The unfinished wing of the hospital can't be that bad.'

The Baudelaires knocked on the door, which opened almost immediately to reveal one of the oldest men they had ever met, wearing one of the tiniest pairs of glasses they had ever seen. Each lens was scarcely bigger than a green pea, and the man had to squint in order to look at them.

'My eyesight isn't what it used to be,'

he said, 'but you appear to be children. And you're very familiar children, too. I'm certain I've seen your faces somewhere before.'

The Baudelaires looked at one another in panic, not knowing whether to dash out of the room or to try to convince the man he was mistaken.

'We're new volunteers,' Violet said. 'I don't think we've ever met before.'

'Babs assigned us to work in the Library of Records,' Klaus said.

'Well, you've come to the right place,' the old man said with a wrinkled smile. 'My name is Hal, and I've worked here in the Library of Records for more years than I'd like to count. I'm afraid my eyesight isn't what it used to be, so I asked Babs if some volunteers could help me.'

'Wolick,' Sunny said.

'My sister says we're very happy to be of assistance,' Violet said, 'and we are.'

'Well, I'm glad to hear that,' Hal said. 'Because there's a lot of work to be done. Come on in and I'll explain what you have to do.'

59

The Baudelaires walked through the door and found themselves in a small room with nothing much in it but a small table that held a bowl of fresh fruit. 'This is the library?' Klaus said.

'Oh no,' the man said. 'This is just an ante-chamber, a small room I'm using to store my fruit. If you get hungry during the day, you may help yourself to something out of that bowl. Also, this is where the intercom is, so we'll have to report here whenever Babs makes an announcement.' He led them across the room to a small door and took a loop of string out of the pocket of his coat. On the loop of string were hundreds of keys, which made tiny clanging noises as they jostled one another. Hal quickly found the right key to unlock the door. 'This,' he said with a small smile, 'is the Library of Records.'

Hal ushered the children inside a dim room with very low ceilings—so low that Hal's gray hair almost brushed against the top. But although the room was not very tall, it was enormous. The Library of Records stretched out so far in front of the Baudelaires that they could scarcely see the opposite wall, or, as the children looked from side to side, the right and left walls. All they could see were big metal file cabinets, with neatly labeled drawers describing the files contained inside. The file cabinets were placed in row after row, as far as the eye could see. The rows were placed very close together, so that the siblings had to walk behind Hal in single file as he gave them the tour of the room.

'I've organized everything myself,' he explained. 'The Library of Records contains information not only from Heimlich Hospital, but from all over the area. There's information about everything from poetry to pills, from picture frames to pyramids, and from pudding to psychology—and that's just in the P aisle, which we're walking down right now.'

'What an amazing place,' Klaus said. 'Just think of everything we can learn from reading all these files.'

'No, no, no,' Hal said, shaking his head sternly. 'We're supposed to file this information, not read it. I don't want to see you touching any of these files except when you're working with them. That's why I keep all these file cabinets locked up tight. Now, let me show you exactly where you'll be working.'

Hal led them to the far wall and pointed out a small rectangular hole, just wide enough for Sunny or maybe Klaus to crawl through. Beside the hole was a basket with a large stack of paper in it, and a bowl filled with paper clips. 'Authorities deposit information into the information chute, which begins outside the hospital and ends right here,' he explained, 'and I need two people to help me file these deposits in the right place. Here's what you do. First, you remove the paper clips and put them in this bowl. Then you glance at the information and figure out where it goes. Remember, try to read as little as possible.' He paused, unclipped a small stack of paper, and squinted at the top page. 'For instance,' he continued. 'You only have to read a few words to see that these paragraphs are about the weather last week at Damocles Dock, which is on the shore of some lake someplace. So you would ask me to unlock cabinets in aisle D, for Damocles, or W, for weather, or even P, for paragraphs. It's your choice.'

'But won't it be difficult for people to find that information again?' Klaus asked. 'They won't know whether to look under D, W, or P.'

'Then they'll have to look under all three letters,' Hal said. 'Sometimes the information you need is not in the most obvious place. Remember, paperwork is the most important thing we do at this hospital, so your job is very important. Do you think you can file these papers correctly? I'd like you to start right away.'

'I think we can,' Violet said. 'But what will the third volunteer do?'

Hal looked embarrassed and held up the loop of string with all the keys on it. 'I lost some of the keys to the file cabinets,' he admitted, 'and I need someone to use some sort of sharp object to open them up.'

'Me!' Sunny said.

'My sister means that she'd be perfect for that job, because she has very sharp teeth,' Violet explained.

'Your sister?' Hal said, and scratched his head. 'Somehow, I knew you three children were from the same family. I'm certain I was just reading some information about you.'

The children looked at one another again, and felt a nervous flutter in their stomachs. 'Do you read *The Daily Punctilio?*' Klaus asked carefully.

'Of course not,' Hal said with a frown. 'That newspaper is the worst I've ever seen. Nearly every story they print is an absolute lie.'

The Baudelaires smiled in relief. 'We can't tell you how happy we are to hear that,' Violet said. 'Well, I guess we'd better get to work.'

'Yes, yes,' Hal said. 'Come on, little one, I'll show you where the locked cabinets are, and you two start filing. I just wish I could remember . . .' The old man's voice trailed off, and then he snapped his fingers and grinned.

There are many reasons, of course,

why someone might snap their fingers and grin. If you heard some pleasing music, for instance, you might snap your fingers and grin to demonstrate that the music had charms that could soothe your savage breast. If you were employed as a spy, you might snap your fingers and grin in order to deliver a message in secret snapping-and-grinning code. But you might also snap your fingers and grin if you had been trying hard to remember something, and had suddenly succeeded. Hal was not listening to music in the Library of Records, and after nine months, six days, and fourteen hours of research, I can say with reasonable certainty that Hal was not employed as a spy, so it would be sensible to conclude he had just remembered something.

'I just remembered something,' he said. 'I know why you three seem so familiar.' Hal continued to lead Sunny down another aisle of file cabinets to show her where her teeth could be handy, so his voice floated over to the two older Baudelaires as if he were speaking on an intercom. 'I didn't read it, of course, but there was some information about you in the file about the Snicket fires.'

CHAPTER
FIVE

'I just don't understand it,' said Klaus, which was not something he said very often.

Violet nodded in agreement, and then said something she didn't say very frequently either. 'It's a puzzle I'm not sure we can solve.'

'Pietrisycamollaviadelrechiotemexity,' Sunny said, which was something she had said only once before. It meant something along the lines of 'I must admit I don't have the faintest idea of what is going on,' and the first time the youngest Baudelaire had said it, she had just been brought home from the hospital where she was born, and was looking at her siblings as they leaned over her crib to greet her. This time, she was sitting in the unfinished wing of the hospital where she worked, and was looking at her siblings as they tried to guess what Hal had meant when he had mentioned 'the Snicket fires.' If I had been with the children, I would have been able to tell them a long and terrible story about men and women who joined a noble organization only to find their lives wrecked by a greedy man and a lazy newspaper, but the siblings were alone, and all they had of the story were a few pages from the Quagmire notebooks.

It was night, and after working all day in the Library of Records, the Baudelaire orphans had made themselves as comfortable as they could in the half-finished section of Heimlich Hospital, but I'm sorry to say the phrase 'as comfortable as they could' here means 'not very comfortable at all.' Violet had found a few flashlights designed to be used by builders working in dark corners, but when she arranged them to light up their surroundings, the light only made clear just how filthy their surroundings really were. Klaus had found some drop-cloths, designed to be used by painters who did not want to drip paint on the floor, but when he wrapped them around himself and his sisters, the warmth only made clear just how freezing it was when the evening wind blew through the sheets of plastic that were nailed to the wooden boards. And Sunny had used her teeth to chop up some of the fruit in Hal's bowl, to make a sort of fruit salad for dinner, but each handful of chopped fruit only made clear just how inappropriate it was to be living in such a bare and lonely place. But even though it was clear to the children how filthy, freezing, and inappropriate their new living quarters were, nothing else seemed clear at all.

'We wanted to use the Library of Records to learn more about Jacques Snicket,' Violet said, 'but we might end up learning more about ourselves.

What in the world do you think is written about us in that file Hal mentioned?'

'I don't know,' Klaus replied, 'and I don't think Hal knows, either. He said he doesn't read any of the files.'

'Seerg,' Sunny said, which meant 'And I was afraid to ask him any more about it.'

'Me, too,' Violet said. 'We simply can't call attention to ourselves. Any minute now, Hal could learn that we're wanted for murder, and we'd be dragged off to jail before we learned anything more.'

'We've already escaped from one jail cell,' Klaus said. 'I don't know if we could do it again.'

'I thought that if we had a chance to look over these pages from Duncan's and Isadora's notebooks,' Violet said, 'we would find the answers to our questions, but the Quagmires' notes are very difficult to read.'

Klaus frowned, and moved a few fragments of the Quagmire pages around as if they were pieces of a jigsaw puzzle. 'The harpoon gun tore these pages to shreds,' he said. 'Look what Duncan has written here: "Jacques Snicket worked for V.F.D., which stands for Volunteer—" and then it's ripped, right in the middle of the sentence.'

'And on this page,' Violet said, picking up a page I cannot bear to think about, 'it reads,

In photographs, and in each public place,
Snicket rarely shows his face.

Isadora must have written that one—it's a rhyming couplet.'

'This scrap says "apartment,"' Klaus said, 'and has what looks like half of a map. That might have to do with the apartment where we lived with Jerome and Esmé Squalor.'

'Don't remind me,' Violet said, shuddering at the thought of all the misfortune the children had encountered at 667 Dark Avenue.

'Rabave,' Sunny said, pointing to one of the pieces of paper.

'This page has two names on it,'

Violet said. 'One name is Al Funcoot.'

'That's the man who wrote that horrible play Olaf forced us to perform,' Klaus said.

'I know,' Violet said, 'but the other name I don't recognize: "Ana Gram."'

'Well, the Quagmires were researching Count Olaf and his sinister plot,' Klaus said. 'Maybe Ana Gram is one of Olaf's associates.'

'It's probably not the hook-handed man,' Violet said, 'or the bald man with the long nose. Ana is not usually a man's name.'

'It could be the name of one of the white-faced women,' Klaus said.

'Orlando!' Sunny said, which meant 'Or the one who looks like neither a man nor a woman.'

'Or someone we haven't even met yet,' Violet said with a sigh, and turned her attention to another piece of paper. 'This page isn't ripped at all, but all it has on it is a long list of dates. It looks like something was going on every twelve weeks or so.'

Klaus picked up the smallest piece and held it up for his sisters to see.

Behind his glasses his eyes looked very sad. 'This piece just says "fire,"' he said quietly, and the three Baudelaires looked down sadly at the dusty floor. With any word, there are subconscious associations, which simply means that certain words make you think of certain things, even if you don't want to. The word 'cake,' for example, might remind you of your birthday, and the words 'prison warden' might remind you of someone you haven't seen in a very long time. The word 'Beatrice' reminds me of a volunteer organization that was swarming with corruption, and the word 'midnight' reminds me that I must keep writing this chapter very quickly, or else I will probably drown. But the Baudelaires had all sorts of subconscious associations with the word 'fire,' and none of them were pleasant to think about. The word made the children think of Hal, who had mentioned something about the Snicket fires that afternoon in the Library of Records. 'Fire' made the youngsters think of Duncan and Isadora Quagmire, who had lost their parents and their brother, Quigley, in a fire. And, of course, the word 'fire' made the Baudelaires think of the fire that had destroyed their home and had begun the unfortunate journey that had led them to the half-finished wing of Heimlich Hospital. The three children huddled quietly together under their drop-cloths, getting colder and colder as they thought about all the fires and subconscious associations that were in the Baudelaire lives.

'That file must contain the answers to all these mysteries,' Violet said finally. 'We need to find out who Jacques Snicket was, and why he had the same tattoo as Count Olaf.'

'And we need to know why he was murdered,' Klaus added, 'and we need to learn the secret of V.F.D.'

'Us,' Sunny said, which meant 'And we need to know why there's a picture of us in the file.'

'We have to get our hands on that file,' Violet said.

'That's easier said than done,' Klaus pointed out. 'Hal told us specifically not to touch any of the files we weren't

74

working with, and he'll be right there with us in the Library of Records.'

'We'll just have to find a way,' Violet replied. 'Now, let's try and get a good night's sleep, so we can stay alert tomorrow, and get ahold of the file on the Snicket fires.'

Klaus and Sunny nodded in agreement, and arranged the drop-cloths into a sort of bed, while Violet turned off the flashlights one by one. The three Baudelaires huddled together for the rest of the night, getting what sleep they could on a filthy floor with a cold wind blowing through their inappropriate home, and in the morning, after a breakfast of leftover fruit salad, they walked to the completed half of Heimlich Hospital and carefully walked down all those stairs, past the intercom speakers and the confusing maps. Hal was already in the Library of Records when they arrived, unlocking the file cabinets with his long loop of keys, and immediately Violet and Klaus got to work filing the information that had come through the chute during the night, while Sunny turned her teeth's attention to the file cabinets that needed to be opened. But the Baudelaires' minds were not on filing, or on file cabinets. Their minds were on the file.

Just about everything in this world is easier said than done, with the exception of 'systematically assisting Sisyphus's stealthy, cyst-susceptible sister,' which is easier done than said. But it is frustrating to be reminded of this fact. As Violet filed a piece of paper containing information on cuttlefish under M, for mollusks, she said to herself, 'I'll just walk down the S aisle and look under Snicket,' but Hal was already in the S aisle, filing away paintings of sewing machines, and she could not do what she said. As Klaus filed a survey of thimbles under P, for protection of the thumb, he said to himself, 'I'll just walk down the F aisle and look under F, for "fires,"' but by that time Hal had moved to the F aisle, and was opening a file cabinet to rearrange biographies of famous Finnish fishermen. And Sunny twisted her teeth this way and that, trying to open one of the locked file cabinets in the B aisle, thinking that perhaps the file was inside, filed under Baudelaires, but when the lock finally broke just after lunch, the youngest sibling opened the cabinet and saw that it was absolutely empty.

'Nil,' Sunny said, as the three children took a short fruit break in the antechamber.

'Me neither,' Klaus said. 'But how can we get ahold of the file, when Hal is always around?'

'Maybe we can just ask him to find it for us,' Violet said. 'If this were a regular library, we would ask the librarian for help. In a Library of Records, maybe we should ask Hal.'

'You can ask me anything you want,' Hal said, walking into the antechamber 'but first I have to ask you something.' He walked over to the children and pointed at one of the fruits. 'Is that a plum or a persimmon?' he asked. 'My eyesight isn't what it used to be, I'm afraid.'

'It's a plum,' Violet said, handing it to him.

'Oh good,' Hal replied, looking it over for bruises. 'I was not in the mood for a persimmon. Now, what is your question?'

'We had a question about a certain file,' Klaus began carefully, not wanting Hal to become suspicious. 'I know it's not customary for us to read the files, but if we were very curious, would it be O.K. to make an exception?'

Hal bit into the plum and frowned. 'Why would you want to read one of the files?' he asked. 'Children should read happy books with bright pictures, not official information from the Library of Records.'

'But we're interested in official information,' Violet said, 'and we're so busy filing things away that we don't get a chance to read anything in the files. That's why we were hoping to take one home with us and read it.'

Hal shook his head. 'Paperwork is the most important thing we do in this hospital,' he said sternly. 'That's why the files are only allowed out of the room if there's a very important reason. For example—'

But the Baudelaires did not get to hear an example, because Hal was interrupted by a voice coming over the intercom. 'Attention!' the voice said, and the children turned to face a small square speaker. 'Attention! Attention!'

The three siblings looked at one another in shock and horror, and then at the wall where the speaker was hanging. The voice coming over the intercom was not Babs's. It was a faint voice, and it was a scratchy voice, but it was not the voice of the Head of Human Resources at Heimlich Hospital. It was a voice that the Baudelaires heard wherever they went, no matter where they lived or who tried to protect them, and even though the children had heard this voice so many times before, they had never gotten used to its sneering tone, as if the person talking were telling a joke with a horrible and violent punch line. 'Attention!' the voice said again, but the orphans did not have to be told to pay attention to the terrible voice of Count Olaf.

'Babs has resigned from Heimlich

Hospital,' said the voice, and the siblings felt as if they could see the cruel smile Olaf always had on his face when he was telling lies. 'She decided to pursue a career as a stuntwoman, and has begun throwing herself off buildings immediately. My name is Mattathias, and I am the new Head of Human Resources. I will be conducting a complete inspection of every single employee here at Heimlich Hospital, beginning immediately. That is all.'

'An inspection,' Hal repeated, finishing his plum. 'What nonsense. They should finish the other half of this hospital, instead of wasting time inspecting everything.'

'What happens during an inspection?' Violet asked.

'Oh, they just come and look you over,' Hal said carelessly, and began walking back to the Library of Records. 'We'd better get back to work. There is a lot more information to file.'

'We'll be along in a moment,' Klaus promised. 'I'm not quite done with my fruit.'

'Well, hurry up,' Hal said, and left the ante-room. The Baudelaires looked at one another in worry and dismay.

'He's found us again,' Violet said, talking quietly so Hal could not hear them. She could barely hear her own voice over the sound of her heart pounding with fear.

'He must know we're here,' Klaus agreed. 'That's why he's doing the inspection—so he can find us and snatch us away.'

'Tell!' Sunny said.

'Who can we tell?' Klaus asked. 'Everyone thinks Count Olaf is dead. They won't believe three children if we say that he's disguised himself as Mattathias, the new Head of Human Resources.'

'Particularly three children who are on the front page of *The Daily Punctilio*,' Violet added, 'wanted for murder. Our only chance is to get that file on the Snicket fires, and see if it has any evidence that will bring Olaf to justice.'

'But files aren't allowed out of the

Library of Records,' Klaus said.

'Then we'll have to read them right here,' Violet said.

'That's easier said than done,' Klaus pointed out. 'We don't even know what letter to look under, and Hal will be right in the room with us all day long.'

'Night!' Sunny said.

'You're right, Sunny,' Violet said. 'Hal is here all day long, but he goes home at night. When it gets dark, we'll sneak back over here from the half-finished wing. It's the only way we'll be able to find the file.'

'You're forgetting something,' Klaus said. 'The Library of Records will be locked up tight. Hal locks all of the file cabinets, remember?'

'I hadn't thought of that,' Violet admitted. 'I can invent one lockpick, but I'm not sure I'll have time to invent enough lockpicks to work on all those file cabinets.'

'Deashew!' Sunny said, which meant something like 'And it takes me several hours to open one cabinet with my teeth!'

'Without the keys, we'll never get the

file,' Klaus said, 'and without the file, we'll never defeat Count Olaf. What can we do?'

The children sighed, and thought as hard as they could, staring in front of them as they did so, and as soon as they stared in front of them they saw something that gave them an idea. The thing they saw was small, and round, and had colorful and shiny skin, and the youngsters could see that it was a persimmon. But the Baudelaires knew that if someone's eyesight wasn't what it used to be, it might look like a plum. The Baudelaire orphans sat and stared at the persimmon, and began to think how they might fool someone into thinking one thing was really another.

CHAPTER SIX

This is not a tale of Lemony Snicket. It is useless to tell the Snicket story, because it happened so very long ago, and because there is nothing anybody can do about the way it has turned out, so the only reason I could possibly have for jotting it down in the margins of these pages would be to make this book even more unpleasant, unnerving, and unbelievable than it already is. This is a story about Violet, Klaus, and Sunny Baudelaire, and how they discovered something in the Library of Records of Heimlich Hospital that changed their lives forever and still gives me the heebie-jeebies whenever I am alone at night STOP. But if this were a book about me, instead of about the three children who would soon run into someone they had hoped never to see again, I might pause for a moment and tell you about something I did many years ago that still troubles me. It was a necessary thing to do, but it was not a nice thing, and even now, I get a small quiver of shame in my stomach whenever I remember it. I might be doing something I enjoy—walking along the promenade deck of a ship, or looking through a telescope at the aurora borealis, or wandering into a bookstore and placing my books on the highest place in the shelf, so that no one will be tempted to buy and read them—when I will suddenly remember this thing I did, and think to myself, *Was it really necessary? Was it absolutely necessary to steal that sugar bowl from Esmé Squalor?*

The Baudelaire orphans were experiencing similar quivers that afternoon, as they finished up the day's work in the Library of Records. Every time Violet put a file in its proper place, she would feel her hair ribbon in her pocket, and get a quiver in her stomach as she thought about what she and her siblings were up to. Klaus would take a stack of papers from the basket in front of the deposit chute, and instead of placing the paper clips in the small bowl, he would keep them hidden in his hand, feeling a quiver in his stomach as he thought about the trick he and his sisters were going to play. And whenever Hal turned his back, and Klaus passed the paper clips to Sunny, the youngest Baudelaire felt a quiver in her stomach as she thought about the sneaky way they were going to return to the Library of Records that night. By the time Hal was locking up the file cabinets for the day with his long loop of keys, the three Baudelaire children had enough quivers in their stomach to attend a Quivery Stomach Festival, if there had been one in the area that afternoon.

'Is it absolutely necessary to do this?' Violet murmured to Klaus, as the three children followed Hal out of the library into the anteroom. She took her hair ribbon out of her pocket and smoothed it out, making sure it didn't have any tangles. 'It's not a nice thing to do.'

'I know,' Klaus answered, holding his hand out so Sunny could hand back the paper clips. 'I have a quiver in my stomach just thinking about it. But it's the only way we can get our hands on that file.'

'Olaf,' Sunny said grimly. She meant 'Before Mattathias gets his hands on us,' and as soon as she was finished with her sentence, Mattathias's scratchy voice came over the intercom.

'Attention! Attention!' the voice said, as Hal and the Baudelaires looked up at the square speaker. 'This is Mattathias, the new Head of Human Resources. Inspections are over for the day but will continue tomorrow.'

'What nonsense,' Hal muttered, putting the loop of keys down on the table. The Baudelaires looked at one another, and then at the keys, as Mattathias continued his announcement.

'Also,' the speaker said, 'if anyone in the hospital has any valuables of any kind, please bring them to the Human Resources office for safekeeping.

Thank you.'

'My eyeglasses are somewhat valuable,' Hal said, taking them off, 'but I'm not going to bring them to the Human Resources office. I might not ever see them again.'

'That's probably true,' Violet said, shaking her head at Mattathias's audacity, a word which here means 'attempt to steal valuables from hospital employees, in addition to snatching the Baudelaire fortune.'

'Besides,' Hal said, smiling at the children and reaching for his coat, 'nobody's going to steal anything from me. You three are the only people I see at the hospital, and I trust you absolutely. Now, where did I put my keys?'

'Here they are,' Violet said, and the quiver in her stomach got worse. She held up her hair ribbon, which had been tied into a circle to look like a loop of string. Hanging from the ribbon was a long row of paper clips, which Sunny had fashioned into different shapes with her teeth when Hal wasn't looking. The result looked something like Hal's loop of keys, the way a horse looks something like a cow, or a woman in a green dress looks something like a pine tree, but there was no way anyone would look at Violet's hair ribbon full of chewed-up paper clips and think it was a ring of keys—unless, of course, their eyesight was not what it used to be. The three children waited as Hal squinted at what Violet was holding.

'Those are my keys?' Hal said doubtfully. 'I thought I put them down on the table.'

'Oh, no,' Klaus said quickly, standing in front of the table so Hal wouldn't catch a glimpse of his real keys. 'Violet has them.'

'Here,' Violet said, moving them back and forth so they would be even harder to squint at, 'why don't I put them in your coat pocket for you?'

'Thank you,' Hal said, as Violet dropped them into his overcoat pocket. He looked at the Baudelaires, his tiny eyes shining with gratitude. 'That's another way you three have helped me. My eyesight's not what it used to be, you know, so I'm glad I can rely on such good volunteers. Well, good night, children. I'll see you tomorrow.'

'Good night, Hal,' Klaus replied. 'We're just going to have one last piece of fruit here in the anteroom.'

'Don't spoil your dinner,' Hal said. 'It's supposed to be a very cold evening, so I bet your parents have cooked up a nice hot meal.' Hal smiled and shut the door behind him, leaving the children alone with the real keys to the Library of Records and the quivery feeling still in their stomachs.

'Someday,' Violet said quietly, 'we'll apologize to Hal for playing a trick on him, and explain why we had to break the rules. This wasn't a nice thing to do, even though it was necessary.'

'And we'll return to the Last Chance General Store,' Klaus said, 'and explain to the shopkeeper why we had to run away.'

'Twisp,' Sunny said firmly, which meant 'But not until we get ahold of the file, solve all these mysteries, and prove our innocence.'

'You're right, Sunny,' Violet said,

with a sigh. 'Let's get started. Klaus, see if you can find the right key for the Library door.'

Klaus nodded, and carried Hal's keys over to the door. Not too long ago, when the Baudelaires had been staying with Aunt Josephine by the shores of Lake Lachrymose, Klaus had been in a situation in which he had to match up a key to a locked door very, very quickly, and since then he had been quite good at it. He looked at the lock of the door, which had a very short and narrow keyhole, and then looked at the loop of string, which had one very short and narrow key, and in no time at all the children were re-entering the Library of Records and looking down the dim aisles of file cabinets.

'I'm going to lock the door behind us,' Klaus said, 'so that nobody will get suspicious if they happen to walk into the anteroom.'

'Like Mattathias,' said Violet with a shudder. 'On the intercom he said that they were stopping the inspections for the day, but I bet he's really still looking.'

'Vapey,' Sunny said, which meant 'Then let's hurry.'

'Let's start with the S aisle,' Violet said. 'For Snicket.'

'Right,' Klaus said, locking the door with a rattle. The three children found the S aisle and began walking past the file cabinets, reading the labels on them to figure out which one to open. 'Sauce to Saxifrage,' Klaus read out loud. 'That means that anything that falls alphabetically between the word "sauce" and the word "saxifrage" will be in this cabinet. That would be fine if we wanted the Sawmill file.'

'Or the Sauna file,' Violet said. 'Let's move on.'

The children moved on, their footsteps echoing off the low ceilings of the room. 'Scarab to Scavenger,' Klaus said, reading one farther down the aisle. Sunny and Violet shook their heads, and the Baudelaires kept moving.

'Secretary to Sediment,' Violet read. 'We're still not there.'

'Kalm,' Sunny said, which meant 'I can't read very well, but I think this one

92

says "Sequel to Serenity.'

'You're right, Sunny,' Klaus said, smiling at his sister. 'It's the wrong one.'

'Shed to Sheepshank,' Violet read.

'Shellac to Sherbet,' Klaus read, walking farther down the aisle.

'Shipwreck to Shrimp.'

'Sicily to Sideways.'

'Skylight to Slob.'

'Sludge to Smoke.'

'Snack to Snifter.'

'Snowball to Sober.'

'Sonnet to Spackle.'

'Wait!' Klaus cried. 'Back up! Snicket is between Snack and Snifter.'

'You're right,' Violet said, stepping back to find the right cabinet. 'I was so distracted by all the strange file names that I forgot what we were looking for. Here it is, Snack to Snifter. Let's hope the file we're looking for is here.'

Klaus looked at the lock on the file cabinet, and found the right key on Hal's loop on only the third try. 'It should be in the bottom drawer,' Klaus said, 'close to Snifter. Let's look.'

The Baudelaires looked. A snifter is

a type of glass, usually meant for holding brandy, although it is also the term for a strong wind. Plenty of words are close to 'snifter' in the alphabet, and the children found many of them. There was a file on sniffing, which seemed to have many photographs of noses. There was a file on Snell's Law, which states that a ray of light passing from one uniform medium to another produces an identical ratio between the sine of the angle of incidence and the sine of the angle of refraction, which Klaus already knew. There was a file on the inventor of the sneaker, whom Violet admired very much, and one on snicking, which is something Sunny had done many times with her teeth. But there was not a single scrap of paper marked Snicket. The children sighed in disappointment, and shut the drawer of the file cabinet so Klaus could lock it again.

'Let's try the J aisle, for Jacques,' Violet suggested.

'Shh,' Sunny said.

'No, Sunny,' Klaus said gently. 'I don't think the H aisle is a good bet.

Why would Hal have filed it under H?'

'Shh,' Sunny insisted, pointing at the door, and her siblings knew instantly that they had misunderstood her. Usually when Sunny said 'Shh,' she meant something along the lines of 'I think the H aisle might be a good place to look for the file,' but this time she meant something more along the lines of 'Be quiet! I think I hear someone walking into the anteroom of the Library of Records.' Sure enough, when the Baudelaires listened closely, they could hear the clomping of some odd, teetering footsteps, as if someone were walking on very thin stilts. The footsteps grew closer and closer, and then stopped, and as the three children held their breath, the door to the Library rattled as someone tried to open the door.

'Maybe it's Hal,' Violet whispered, 'trying to unlock the door with a paper clip.'

'Maybe it's Mattathias,' Klaus whispered, 'looking for us.'

'Janitor,' Sunny whispered.

'Well, whoever it is,' Violet said,

95

'we'd better hurry to the J aisle.'

The Baudelaires tiptoed across the low-ceilinged room to the J aisle, and walked down it quickly, reading the labels of the file cabinets.

'Jabberwocky to Jackal.'

'Jacket to Jack-o'-Lanterns.'

'Nersai.'

'That's it!' Klaus whispered. 'Jacques will be in Jackline to Jacutinga.'

'We hope,' Violet said, as the door rattled again. Klaus hurried to find the right key, and the children opened the top drawer to look for Jacques. As Violet knew, jackline is a kind of rope used in sailing, and as Klaus knew, jacutinga is a sort of gold-bearing iron ore found in Brazil, and once again there were plenty of files between these two, but although the children found information on jack-o'-lanterns, Jack Russell terriers, and Jacobean drama, there was no file marked 'Jacques.'

'Fire!' Klaus whispered, shutting and locking the file cabinet. 'Let's head to the F aisle.'

'And hurry,' Violet said. 'It sounds

like the person in the anteroom is picking the lock.'

It was true. The Baudelaires paused for a moment and heard a muffled scratching from behind the door, as if something long and thin were being stuck in the keyhole to try to unlock the lock. Violet knew, from when she and her siblings lived with Uncle Monty, that a lockpick can often take a long time to work properly, even if it has been made by one of the world's greatest inventors, but the children nonetheless moved to the F aisle as fast as their tiptoes could carry them.

'Fabian to Fact.'

'Fainting to Fangs.'

'Fatalism to Faulkner.'

'Fear to Fermat.'

'Ficus to Filth.'

'Fin de Siecle to Fissle—here it is!'

Once more, the Baudelaires hurried to find the proper key, and then the proper drawer and then the proper file. 'Fin de siecle' is a term for a time in history when a century is drawing to a close, and 'fissle' is a fancy word for a rustling noise, like the one that continued to come from behind the locked door as the children looked frantically for Fire. But the papers went right from Finland to Firmament, without a single word on Fire in between.

'What will we do?' Violet asked, as the door began to rattle again. 'Where else could the file be?'

'Let's try to think,' Klaus said. 'What did Hal say about the file? We know it has to do with Jacques Snicket, and with fire.'

'Prem!' Sunny said, which meant 'But we looked under Snicket, Jacques, and Fire already.'

'There must be something else,' Violet said. 'We have to find this file. It has crucial information about Jacques Snicket and V.F.D.'

'And about us,' Klaus said. 'Don't forget that.'

The three children looked at one another.

'Baudelaire!' Sunny whispered.

Without another word, the orphans ran to the B aisle, and hurried past Babbitt to Babylon, Bacteria to Ballet, and Bamboo to Baskerville, stopping at Bat Mitzvah to Bavarian Cream. As the door continued to fissle behind them, Klaus tried nine keys in a row before finally opening the cabinet, and there, between the Jewish coming-of-age ceremony for young women, and the delicious filling of certain doughnuts, the children found a folder marked 'Baudelaire.'

'It's here,' Klaus said, taking it out of the drawer with trembling hands.

'What does it say? What does it say?' Violet asked in excitement.

'Look,' Klaus said. 'There's a note on the front.'

'Read it!' Sunny said in a frantic whisper, as the door began to shake violently on its hinges. Whoever was on the other side of the door was obviously getting frustrated with trying to pick the lock.

Klaus held up the file so he could see what the note said in the dim light of the room. '"All thirteen pages of the Snicket file,' he read, '"have been removed from the Library of Records for the official investigation."' He looked up at his sisters, and they could see that, behind his glasses, his eyes were filling with tears. 'That must be when Hal saw our picture,' he said. 'When he removed the file and gave it to the official investigators.' He dropped the file on the floor and then sat down beside it in despair. 'There's nothing here.'

'Yes there is!' Violet said. 'Look!'

The Baudelaires looked at the file where Klaus had dropped it on the ground. There, behind the note, was a single sheet of paper. 'It's page thirteen,' Violet said, looking at a number typed in a corner of the paper. 'The investigators must have left it behind by mistake.'

'That's why you should keep paper clips on papers that belong together,' Klaus said, 'even when you file them. But what does the page say?'

With a long *crackle!* and a loud *bang,* the door to the Library of Records was knocked off its hinges, and fell to the floor of the enormous room as if it had fainted. But the children paid no attention. Violet, Klaus, and Sunny all sat and looked at page thirteen of the file, too amazed to even listen to the odd, teetering footsteps as the intruder entered the room and began to walk along the aisles of file cabinets.

Page thirteen of the Baudelaire file was not a crowded sheet of paper— there was just one photograph stapled into place, below one sentence of type. But sometimes it takes only a photograph and a sentence to make an author cry himself to sleep even years after the photograph was taken, or to make three siblings sit and stare at a page for a long time, as if an entire book were printed on one sheet of paper.

There were four people in the photograph, standing together outside a building the Baudelaires recognized immediately. It was 667 Dark Avenue, where the orphans had lived with Jerome and Esmé Squalor for a brief time, until it became another place too treacherous for the children to stay. The first person in the photograph was Jacques Snicket, who was looking at the photographer and smiling.

Standing next to Jacques was a man who was turned away from the camera, so the children could not see his face, only one of his hands, which was clutching a notebook and pen, as if the obscured man were a writer of some sort. The children had not seen Jacques Snicket since he was murdered, of course, and the writer appeared to be someone they had never seen at all. But standing next to these two people were another two people the Baudelaire children thought they would never see again. Bundled up in long coats, looking cold but happy, were the Baudelaire parents.

'Because of the evidence discussed on page nine,' read the sentence above the photograph, 'experts now suspect that there may in fact be one survivor of the fire, but the survivor's whereabouts are unknown.'

CHAPTER SEVEN

'I never thought I'd live to see the day,' Violet said, and took another look at page thirteen of the file. The Baudelaire parents looked back at her, and for a moment it seemed to Violet her father would step out of the photograph and say, 'There you are, Ed. Where have you been?' Ed was short for Thomas Alva Edison, one of the greatest inventors of all time, and it was a special nickname only used by her father, but the man in the photograph did not move, of

103

course, but only stood smiling in front of 667 Dark Avenue.

'Me neither,' Klaus said. 'I never thought we'd see our parents again.' The middle Baudelaire looked at his mother's coat, which had a secret pocket on the inside. In the secret pocket, she often kept a small pocket dictionary, which she would take out whenever she encountered a word she did not know. Because Klaus was so interested in reading, she had promised that someday she would give the pocket dictionary to him, and now it seemed to Klaus that his mother was about to reach into her coat and put the small, leatherbound book in his hand.

'Neither me,' Sunny said. She looked at her parents' smiles, and suddenly remembered, for the first time since the fire, a song that her mother and father used to sing together, when it was time for Sunny to go to sleep. The song was called 'The Butcher Boy,' and the Baudelaire parents would take turns singing the verses, her mother singing in her breathy, high voice, and her father in his, which was as low and deep as a foghorn. 'The Butcher Boy' was the perfect way for Sunny to end the day, safe and cozy in the Baudelaire crib.

'This photograph must have been taken a long time ago,' Violet said. 'Look how much younger they look. They aren't even wearing their wedding rings.'

' "Because of the evidence discussed on page nine,' Klaus said, reading the sentence typed above the photograph, ' "experts now suspect that there may in fact be one survivor of the fire, but the survivor's whereabouts are unknown." ' He stopped, and looked at his sisters. 'What does that mean?' he said, in a very faint voice. 'Does that mean one of our parents is still alive?'

'Well, well, well,' said a familiar and sneering voice, and the children heard the odd, tottering footsteps walk straight toward them. 'Look what we have here.'

The Baudelaire orphans had been so shocked by what they had found that they had forgotten about the person breaking into the Library of Records, and now they looked up to see a tall, skinny figure walking down the B aisle STOP. It was a person they had seen recently, and one they had hoped never to see again. There are many different ways of describing this person, including 'Count Olaf's girlfriend,' 'the Baudelaire children's former guardian,' 'the city's sixth most important financial advisor,' 'a former resident of 667 Dark Avenue,' and several phrases that are far too nasty to be placed in a book. But the name she preferred was the one that came snarling out of her lipsticked mouth.

'I am Esmé Gigi Geniveve Squalor,' said Esmé Gigi Geniveve Squalor, as if the Baudelaires would ever forget her, no matter how hard they tried. She stopped walking and stood in front of the Baudelaires, who saw immediately why her footsteps had been so odd and tottering. For as long as the children had known her, Esmé Squalor had been a slave to fashion, a phrase which here means 'dressed in incredibly expensive, and often incredibly absurd, outfits.' This evening she was wearing a long coat made from the fur of a number of animals that had been killed in particularly unpleasant ways, and she was carrying a handbag shaped like an eye, just like the tattoo her boyfriend had on his left ankle. She wore a hat with a small veil that hung in front of her face, as if she had blown her nose with a black lacy handkerchief, and then forgotten to remove it, and on her feet she had a pair of shoes with stiletto heels. A stiletto is a small, slender knife resembling a dagger, such as might be carried by a carnival performer or a murderer, and the word 'stiletto' has been used to describe a woman's shoe with a very long and narrow heel. In this case, however, the phrase 'shoes with stiletto heels' actually refers to a pair of shoes made with a small, slender knife where each heel should be. The stilettos were pointing straight down, so that Esmé viciously stabbed the floor of the Library of Records with each step, and occasionally the stilettos stuck, so the wicked woman had to pause and yank them out of the floor, which explained why her footsteps were so odd and tottering. These shoes happened to be the absolute latest fashion, but the Baudelaires had more important things to do than leaf through magazines describing what was in and what was out, so they could only stare at Esmé's shoes and wonder why she was wearing footwear that was so violent and impractical.

'This is a pleasant surprise,' Esmé said. 'Olaf asked me to break in here and destroy the Baudelaire file, but now we can destroy the Baudelaires as well.'

The children looked at each other in shock.

'You and Olaf *know* about the file?' Violet asked.

Esmé laughed in a particularly nasty way, and, from behind her veil, smiled a particularly nasty smile. 'Of course we know about it,' she snarled. 'That's why I'm here—to destroy all thirteen pages.' She took one odd, tottering step toward the Baudelaires. 'That's why we destroyed Jacques Snicket.' She took another stabbing step down the aisle. 'And that's why we're going to destroy you.' She looked down at her shoe and shook her foot wildly to get the blade out of the library floor. 'Heimlich Hospital is about to have three new patients,' she said, 'but I'm afraid it'll be too late for any doctor to save their lives.'

Klaus stood up, and followed his sisters as they began to step away from the slave to fashion who was moving slowly toward them. 'Who survived the fire?' he asked Esmé, holding up the page from the file. 'Is one of our parents alive?'

Esmé frowned, and teetered on her stiletto heels as she tried to snatch the page away. *'Did you read the file?'* she demanded in a terrible voice. *'What does the file say?'*

'You'll never find out!' Violet cried, and turned to her siblings. 'Run!'

The Baudelaires ran, straight down the aisle past the rest of the B files, rounding the corner past the cabinet that read 'Byron to Byzantine' and around to the section of the library where all of the C files were stored.

'We're running the wrong way,' Klaus said.

'Egress,' Sunny agreed, which meant something along the lines of, 'Klaus is right—the exit is the other way.'

'So is Esmé,' Violet replied. 'Somehow, we'll have to go around her.'

'I'm coming for you!' Esmé cried, her voice coming over the top of the file cabinets. 'You'll never escape, orphans!'

The Baudelaires paused at the cabinet reading 'Conch to Condy's Fluid,' which are a fancy seashell and a complex chemical compound, and listened as Esmé's heels clattered in pursuit.

'We're lucky she's wearing those ridiculous shoes,' Klaus said. 'We can run much faster than she can.'

'As long as she doesn't think of taking them off,' Violet said. 'She's almost as clever as she is greedy.'

'Shh!' Sunny said, and the Baudelaires listened as Esmé's footsteps abruptly stopped. The children huddled together as they heard Olaf's girlfriend mutter to herself for a moment, and then the three youngsters began to hear a terrifying sequence of sounds. There was a long, screechy *creak*, and then a booming *crash*, and then another long, screechy *creak*, and another booming *crash*, and the pair of sounds continued, getting louder and louder. The youngsters looked at one another in puzzlement, and then, just in the nick of time, the oldest Baudelaire figured out what the sound was.

'She's knocking over the file cabinets!' Violet cried, pointing over the top of Confetti to Consecration. 'They're toppling over like dominos!'

Klaus and Sunny looked where their sister was pointing and saw that she was right. Esmé had pushed over one file cabinet, which had pushed over another, which had pushed over another, and now the heavy metal cabinets were crashing toward the children like a wave crashing on the shore. Violet grabbed her siblings and pulled them out of the path of a falling

111

file cabinet. With *a creak* and a *crash,* the cabinet fell to the floor, right where they had been standing. The three children breathed a sigh of relief, having just narrowly avoided being crushed beneath files on congruent triangles, coniferous trees, conjugated verbs, and two hundred other topics.

'I'm going to flatten you!' Esmé called, starting on another line of cabinets. 'Olaf and I are going to have a romantic breakfast of Baudelaire pancakes!'

'Run!' Sunny cried, but her siblings needed no urging. The three children hurried down the rest of the C aisle, as the cabinets *creaked* and *crashed* all around them.

'Where can we go?' Violet cried.

'To the D aisle!' Klaus answered, but changed his mind as he saw another row of cabinets begin to topple. 'No! The E aisle!'

'B?' Violet asked, finding it difficult to hear over the sounds of the cabinets.

'E!' Klaus cried. 'E as in Exit!'

The Baudelaires ran down E as in Exit, but when they reached the last

cabinet, the row was becoming F as in Falling File Cabinets, G as in Go the Other Way! and H as in How in the World Are We Going to Escape? Before long, the children found themselves as far from the anteroom door as they possibly could be. As the cabinets crashed around them, and Esmé cackled wildly and stabbed the floor in pursuit, the three youngsters found themselves in the area of the Library of Records where information was deposited. As the room *creaked* and *crashed* around them, the siblings looked first at the basket of papers, then at the bowl of paper clips, then the mouth of the chute, and finally at one another.

'Violet,' Klaus said hesitantly, 'do you think you can invent something out of paper clips and a basket that could help us get out of here?'

'I don't have to,' Violet said. 'That chute will serve as an exit.'

'But you won't fit in there,' Klaus said. 'I'm not even sure I will.'

'You're never going to get out of this room alive, you imbeciles!' Esmé cried, using a horrible word in her horrible voice.

'We'll have to try,' Violet said. 'Sunny, go first.'

'Prapil,' Sunny said doubtfully, but she went first, crawling easily into the chute and staring out through the darkness at her siblings.

'Now you, Klaus,' Violet said, and Klaus, removing his glasses so they wouldn't break, followed his sister. It was a tight fit, and it took some maneuvering, but eventually the middle Baudelaire worked his way through the mouth of the chute.

'This won't work,' Klaus said to Violet, peering around him. 'It'll be tough to crawl up through the chute, the way it's slanted. Besides, there's no way you'll fit.'

'Then I'll find another way,' Violet said. Her voice was calm, but Klaus and Sunny could see, through the hole in the wall, that her eyes were wide with fear.

'That's out of the question,' Klaus said. 'We'll climb back out, and the three of us will escape together.'

115

'We can't risk it,' Violet said. 'Esmé won't catch all of us, not if we split up. You two take page thirteen and go up the chute, and I'll get out another way. We'll meet up in the unfinished wing.'

'No!' Sunny cried.

'Sunny's right,' Klaus said. 'This is what happened with the Quagmires, remember? When we left them behind, they were snatched away.'

'The Quagmires are safe now,' Violet reminded him. 'Don't worry, I'll invent a solution.'

The eldest Baudelaire gave her siblings a small smile, and reached into her pocket so she could tie up her hair and put the levers and gears of her inventing mind into motion. But there was no ribbon in her pocket. As her trembling fingers explored her empty pocket, she remembered she had used her ribbon to fool Hal with a fake loop of keys. Violet felt a quiver in her stomach as she remembered, but she had no time to feel bad about the trick she had played. With sudden horror, she heard a *creak* right behind her, and she jumped out of the way just in time

116

to avoid the *crash*. A file cabinet labeled 'Linguistics to Lions' fell against the wall, blocking the mouth of the chute.

'Violet!' Sunny cried. She and her brother tried to push the cabinet aside, but the strength of a thirteen-year-old boy and his baby sister were no match against a metal case holding files on everything from the history of language to a large carnivorous feline found in sub-Saharan Africa and parts of India.

'I'm O.K.,' Violet called back.

'Not for long you're not!' Esmé snarled, from a few aisles over.

Klaus and Sunny sat in the dark chute and heard their sister's faint voice as she called to them. 'Leave me here!' she insisted. 'I'll meet you back in our filthy, cold, inappropriate home.'

The two younger Baudelaires huddled together at the entrance of the chute, but it is useless for me to describe to you how desperate and terrified they felt. There is no reason to describe how horrible it was to hear Violet's frantic footsteps across the Library of Records, or the odd, tottering ones of Esmé as she pursued the eldest Baudelaire in her stiletto heels, *creak*ing and *crash*ing file cabinets with every stabbing step. It is unnecessary to describe the cramped and difficult journey Klaus and Sunny made up the chute, which was slanted so steeply that it felt to the two orphans like they were crawling up a large mountain covered in ice instead of a fairly short chute used for depositing information. It is ineffectual to describe how the two children felt when they finally reached the end of the chute, which was another hole, carved into the outside wall of Heimlich Hospital, and found that Hal was right when he said it was to be a particularly cold evening. And it is absolutely futile—a word which here means 'useless, unnecessary, and ineffectual, because there is no reason for it'—to describe how they felt as they sat in the half-finished section of the hospital, with drop-cloths wrapped around them to keep them warm and flashlights lit around them to keep them company, and waited for Violet to show up, because Klaus and Sunny Baudelaire were not thinking of these things.

The two younger Baudelaires sat together, clutching page thirteen of the Baudelaire file, as the night grew later and later, but they were not thinking about the noises they heard coming from the Library of Records, or about the journey up the chute or even about the icy breeze as it blew through the plastic sheets and chilled the Baudelaire bones. Klaus and Sunny were thinking about what Violet had said, when she saw the piece of paper they were clutching now.

'I never thought I'd live to see the day,' Violet had said, and her two siblings knew that the phrase was just another way of saying 'I'm very surprised' or 'I'm extremely flabbergasted' or 'This blows my mind beyond belief.' But now, as the two Baudelaires waited more and more anxiously for their sister, Klaus and Sunny began to fear that the phrase Violet used was more appropriate than she ever would have guessed. As the first pale rays of the morning sun began to shine on the unfinished half of the hospital, the Baudelaries grew more and more frightened that their sister would not live to see the day.

CHAPTER EIGHT

Heimlich Hospital is gone now, and will probably never be rebuilt. If you want to visit it, you have to convince a farmer to let you borrow his mule, for nobody in the surrounding area is willing to go within twelve miles of its wreckage, and once you arrive you can hardly blame them. The few scraps of the building that have survived are covered with a thick and prickly type of ivy called kudzu, which makes it difficult to see what the hospital looked like when the Baudelaires first arrived in the V.F.D. van. The confusing maps have been gnawed off the walls of the sagging staircases, so it is very hard to imagine how troublesome it was to find one's way through all of the areas of the building. And the intercom system has long since crumbled away, with only a handful of square speakers left sitting among the ashen rubble, so it is impossible to imagine just how unnerving it was when Klaus and Sunny heard the latest announcement from Mattathias.

'Attention!' Mattathias announced. There were no intercom speakers installed in the unfinished half of the hospital, so the two younger Baudelaires had to listen very hard to hear the scratchy voice of their enemy coming from one of the outdoor speakers. 'Attention! Attention! This is Mattathias, the Head of Human Resources. I am canceling the remainder of the hospital inspections. We have found what we were looking for.' There was a pause as Mattathias moved away from the microphone, and as Klaus and Sunny listened very hard, they could hear the faint, faint noise of triumphant, high-pitched laughter coming from the Head of Human Resources.

'Excuse me,' he continued, when his giggling fit was over. 'To continue, please be aware that two of the three Baudelaire murderers—Klaus and Sun —I mean, Klyde and Susie Baudelaire —have been spotted in the hospital. If you see any children whom you recognize from *The Daily Punctilio*, please capture them and notify the police.' Mattathias stopped talking and began to giggle again, until the children heard the voice of Esmé Squalor whispering, 'Darling, you forgot to turn off the intercom.' Then there was a click, and everything was silent.

'They caught her,' Klaus said. Now that the sun had risen, it wasn't very cold in the half-finished section of the hospital, but the middle Baudelaire shivered nonetheless. 'That's what Mattathias meant when he said that they had found what they were looking for.'

'Danger,' Sunny said grimly.

'She certainly is,' Klaus said. 'We have to rescue Violet before it's too late.'

'Virm,' Sunny said, which meant 'But we don't know where she is.'

'She must be somewhere in the

123

hospital,' Klaus said, 'otherwise Mattathias wouldn't still be here. He and Esmé are probably hoping to capture us, too.'

'Rance,' Sunny said.

'And the file,' Klaus agreed, taking page thirteen out of his pocket, where he had been storing it for safekeeping along with the scraps of the Quagmire notebooks. 'Come on, Sunny. We've got to find our sister and get her out of there.'

'Lindersto,' Sunny said. She meant 'That'll be tough. We'll have to wander around the hospital looking for her, while other people will be wandering around the hospital, looking for us.'

'I know,' Klaus said glumly. 'If anyone recognizes us from *The Daily Punctilio*, we'll be in jail before we can help Violet.'

'Disguise?' Sunny said.

'I don't know how,' Klaus said, looking around the half-finished room. 'All we have here is some flashlights and a few drop-cloths. I suppose if we wrapped the drop-cloths around us and put the flashlights on top of our heads, we could try to disguise ourselves as piles of construction materials.'

'Gidoost,' Sunny said, which meant 'But piles of construction materials don't wander around hospitals.'

'Then we'll have to walk into the hospital without disguises,' Klaus said. 'We'll just have to be extra careful.'

Sunny nodded emphatically, a word which here means 'as if she thought being extra careful was a very good plan,' and Klaus nodded emphatically back. But as they left the half-finished wing of the hospital, the two children felt less and less emphatic about what they were doing. Ever since that terrible day at the beach, when Mr. Poe brought them news of the fire, all three Baudelaires had been extra careful all of the time. They had been extra careful when they lived with Count Olaf, and Sunny had still ended up dangling from a cage outside Olaf's tower room. They had been extra careful when they'd worked at the Lucky Smells Lumbermill, and Klaus had still ended up hypnotized by Dr. Orwell. And now the Baudelaires had been as careful as they could possibly be, but the hospital had turned out to be as hostile an environment as anywhere the three children had ever lived. But just as Klaus and Sunny entered the finished half of Heimlich Hospital, their feet moving less and less emphatically and their hearts beating faster and faster, they heard something that soothed their savage breasts:

'We are Volunteers Fighting Disease,
And we're cheerful all day long.
If someone said that we were sad,
That person would be wrong.'

There, coming around the corner, were the Volunteers Fighting Disease, walking down the hall singing their cheerful song and carrying enormous bunches of heart-shaped balloons. Klaus and Sunny looked at one another, and ran to catch up with the group. What better place to hide than among people who believed that no news was good news, and so didn't read the newspaper?

126

'We visit people who are sick,
And try to make them smile,
Even if their noses bleed,
Or if they cough up bile.'

To the children's relief, the volunteers paid no attention as Klaus and Sunny infiltrated the group, a phrase which here means 'sneaked into the middle of a singing crowd.' An especially cheerful singer seemed to be the only one who noticed, and she immediately handed a balloon to each newcomer. Klaus and Sunny held the balloons in front of their faces, so that anybody passing by would see two volunteers with shiny, helium-filled hearts, instead of two accused criminals hiding in V.F.D.

'Tra la la, Fiddle dee dee,
Hope you get well soon.
Ho ho ho, hee hee hee,
Have a heart-shaped balloon.'

As the volunteers reached the chorus of the song, they marched into a hospital room in order to start giving a cheerful attitude to the patients. Inside the room, each lying uncomfortably in a metal bed, were a man with both legs in casts and a woman with both arms in bandages. Still singing, a man from V.F.D. handed one balloon to the man and tied another to the woman's cast, because she could not hold it with her broken arms.

'Excuse me,' said the man hoarsely, 'could you please call a nurse for me? I was supposed to take some painkillers this morning, but nobody has come to give them to me.'

'And I'd like a glass of water,' the woman said in a weak voice, 'if it's not too much trouble.'

'Sorry,' the bearded man replied, pausing for a moment to tune his guitar. 'We don't have time to do things like that. We have to visit each and every room of the hospital, so we need to move quickly.'

'Besides,' another volunteer said, giving the two patients a huge grin, 'a cheerful attitude is a more effective way of fighting illness than painkillers, or a glass of water. So cheer up, and enjoy your balloon.' The volunteer consulted a list he was holding. 'Next on the patient list is a man named Bernard Rieux, in room 105 of the Plague Ward. Come on, brothers and sisters.'

The members of V.F.D. cheered, and continued the song as they left the room. Klaus and Sunny peered around the balloons they were holding and looked at one another in hope.

'If we visit each and every room in the hospital,' Klaus whispered to his sister, 'we're sure to find Violet.'

'Mushulm,' Sunny said, which meant 'I agree, although it won't be pleasant to see all these sick people.'

'We visit people who are ill,
And try to make them laugh,
Even when the doctor says
He must saw them in half.'

Bernard Rieux turned out to be a man with a nasty, hacking cough that shook his body so much he could scarcely hold his balloon, and it seemed to the two Baudelaire children that a good humidifier would have been a more effective way to fight this disease than a cheerful attitude. As the members of V.F.D. drowned out his cough with another verse of the song, Klaus and Sunny were tempted to run and find a humidifier and bring it back to Bernard Rieux's room, but they knew that Violet was in much more danger than someone with a cough, so they stayed hidden in the group.

'We sing and sing all night and day,
And then we sing some more.
We sing to boys with broken bones
And girls whose throats are sore.'

The next patient on the list was Cynthia Vane, a young woman with a terrible toothache who probably would have preferred something cold and easy to eat, instead of a heart-shaped balloon, but as sore as her mouth looked, the children dared not run and find her applesauce or an ice-cream snack. They knew she might have read *The Daily Punctilio*, in order to pass the hours in the hospital room, and might recognize them if they showed their faces.

> *'Tra la la, Fiddle dee dee,*
> *Hope you get well soon.*
> *Ho ho ho, hee hee hee,*
> *Have a heart-shaped balloon.'*

On and on the volunteers marched, and Klaus and Sunny marched with them, but with every *ho ho ho* and *hee hee hee* their hearts sank lower and lower. The two Baudelaires followed the members of V.F.D. up and down the staircases of the hospital, and although they saw a great number of confusing maps, intercom speakers, and sick people, they did not catch a glimpse of their sister. They visited Room 201 and sang to Jonah Mapple, who was suffering from seasickness, and they gave a heart-shaped balloon to Charley Anderson in Room 714, who had injured himself in an accident, and they visited Clarissa Dalloway, who did not seem to have anything wrong with her but was staring sadly out the window of Room 1308, but nowhere, in any of the rooms that the volunteers marched into, was Violet Baudelaire, who, Klaus and Sunny feared, was suffering more than any of the other patients.

'Ceyune,' Sunny said, as the volunteers walked up yet another staircase. She meant something along the lines of 'We've been wandering around the hospital all morning, and we're no closer to rescuing our sister,' and Klaus nodded grimly in agreement.

'I know,' Klaus said, 'but the members of V.F.D. are going to visit every single person in Heimlich Hospital. We're sure to find Violet eventually.'

'Attention! Attention!' a voice announced, and the volunteers stopped singing and gathered around the nearest intercom speaker to hear what Mattathias had to say. 'Attention!' Mattathias said. '"Today is a very important day in the history of the hospital. In precisely one hour, a doctor here will perform the world's first cranioectomy on a fourteen-year-old girl. We all hope that this very dangerous operation is a complete success. That is all.'

'Violet,' Sunny murmured to her brother.

'I think so, too,' Klaus said. 'And I don't like the sound of that operation. "Cranio" means "head," and "ectomy" is a medical term for removing something.'

'Decap?' Sunny asked in a horrified whisper. She meant something like 'Do you think they're going to cut off Violet's head?'

'I don't know,' Klaus said with a shudder, 'but we can't wander around with these singing volunteers any longer. We've got to find her right away.'

'O.K.,' a volunteer called, consulting the list. 'The next patient is Emma Bovary in Room 2611. She has food poisoning, so she needs a particularly cheerful attitude.'

'Excuse me, brother,' Klaus said to the volunteer, reluctantly using the term 'brother' instead of 'person I hardly know.' 'I was wondering if I could borrow your copy of the patient list.'

'Of course,' the volunteer replied. 'I don't like to read all these names of sick people, anyway. It's too depressing. I'd rather hold balloons.' With a cheerful smile, the volunteer handed Klaus the long list of patients, and took the heart-shaped balloon out of his hands as the bearded man began the next verse of the song.

'We sing to men with measles,
And to women with the flu,
And if you breathe in deadly germs,
We'll probably sing to you.'

With his face exposed, Klaus had to duck down behind Sunny's balloon to look at the list of the hospital's patients. 'There are hundreds of people on this list,' he said to his sister, 'and it's organized by ward, not by name. We can't read it all here in the hallway, particularly when we both have to hide behind one balloon.'

'Damajat,' Sunny said, pointing down the hall. By 'Damajat,' she meant

134

something along the lines of 'Let's hide in that supply closet over there,' and sure enough, there was a door marked 'Supply Closet' at the end of the hallway, past two doctors who had paused to chat beside one of the confusing maps. While the members of V.F.D. started in on the chorus of their song as they walked toward Emma Bovary's room, Klaus and Sunny separated themselves from the volunteers and walked carefully toward the closet, holding the balloon in front of both their faces as best they could. Luckily, the two doctors were too busy talking about a sporting event they had watched on television to notice two accused murderers sneaking down the hallway of their hospital, and by the time the volunteers were singing

> 'Tra la la, Fiddle dee dee,
> Hope you get well soon.
> Ho ho ho, hee hee hee,
> Have a heart-shaped balloon.'

Klaus and Sunny were inside the closet. Like a church bell, a coffin, and a vat of melted chocolate, a supply closet is rarely a comfortable place to hide, and this supply closet was no exception. When they shut the door of the closet behind them, the two younger Baudelaires found themselves in a small, cramped room lit only by one flickering lightbulb hanging from the ceiling. On one wall was a row of white medical coats hanging from hooks, and on the opposite wall was a rusty sink where one could wash one's hands before examining a patient. The rest of the closet was full of huge cans of alphabet soup for patients' lunches, and small boxes of rubber bands, which the children could not imagine came in very handy in a hospital.

'Well,' Klaus said, 'it's not comfortable, but at least nobody will find us in here.'

'Pesh,' Sunny said, which meant something like 'At least, until somebody needs rubber bands, alphabet soup, white medical coats, or clean hands.'

'Well, let's keep one eye on the door, to see if anyone comes in,' Klaus said, 'but let's keep the other eye on this list.

It's very long, but now that we have a few moments to look it over, we should be able to spot Violet's name.'

'Right,' Sunny said. Klaus placed the list on top of a can of soup, and hurriedly began to flip through its pages. As he had noticed, the list of patients was not organized alphabetically, but by ward, a word which here means 'particular section of the hospital,' so the two children had to look through every single page, hoping to spot the name Violet Baudelaire among the typed names of sick people. But as they glanced at the list under the heading 'Sore Throat Ward,' perused the names on the 'Broken Neck Ward' page, and combed through the names of all the people who were staying in the Ward for People with Nasty Rashes, Klaus and Sunny felt as if they were in a Ward for People with Sinking Stomachs, because Violet's name was nowhere to be found. As the lightbulb flickered above them, the two Baudelaires looked frantically at page after page of the list, but they found nothing that would help them locate

137

their sister.

'She's not here,' Klaus said, putting down the last page of 'Pneumonia Ward.'

'Violet's name is nowhere on the list. How are we going to find her in this huge hospital, if we can't figure out what ward she's in?'

'Alias,' Sunny said, which meant 'Maybe she's listed under a different name.'

'That's true,' Klaus said, looking at the list again. 'After all, Mattathias's real name is Count Olaf. Maybe he made up a new name for Violet, so we couldn't rescue her. But which person is really Violet? She could be anyone from Mikhail Bulgakov to Haruki Murakami. What are we going to do? Somewhere in this hospital, they're getting ready to perform a completely unnecessary operation on our sister, and we—'

Klaus was interrupted by the sound of crackly laughter, coming from over the Baudelaires' heads. The two children looked up and saw that a square intercom speaker had been installed on the ceiling. 'Attention!' said Mattathias, when he was done laughing. 'Dr. Flacutono, please report to the Surgical Ward. Dr. Flacutono, please report to the Surgical Ward to prepare for the cranioectomy.'

'Flacutono!' Sunny repeated.

'I recognize that name, too,' Klaus said. 'That's the false name used by Count Olaf's associate when we lived in Paltryville.'

'Tiofreck!' Sunny said frantically. She meant 'Violet's in grave danger—we have to find her immediately,' but Klaus did not answer. Behind his glasses, his eyes were half closed, as they often were when he was trying to remember something he had read.

'Flacutono,' he muttered quietly. 'Flac-uto-no.' Then he reached into his pocket, where he was keeping all the important papers the Baudelaires had gathered. 'Al Funcoot,' he said, and took out one of the pages of the Quagmire notebooks. It was the page that had written on it the words 'Ana Gram'—a phrase that had not made

139

any sense to the Baudelaires when they had looked at the pages together. Klaus looked at the Quagmire page, and then at the list of patients, and then at the page again. Then he looked at Sunny, and she could see his eyes grow wide behind his glasses, the way they always did when he had read something very difficult, and understood it at last.

'I think I know how to find Violet,' Klaus said slowly, 'but we'll need your teeth, Sunny.'

'Ready,' Sunny said, opening her mouth.

Klaus smiled, and pointed to the stack of cans in the supply closet. 'Open one of those cans of alphabet soup,' he said, 'and hurry.'

CHAPTER
Nine

'Recazier?' Sunny asked dumbfoundedly. The word 'dumbfoundedly' here means 'wondering why in the world Klaus wanted to eat alphabet soup at a time like this,' and 'Recazier?' here means 'Klaus, why in the world do you want to eat alphabet soup at a time like this?'

'We're not going to eat it,' Klaus said, handing Sunny one of the cans. 'We're going to pour just about all of it down the sink.'

'Pietrisycamollaviadelrechiotemexity,' Sunny said, which you will probably recall means something along the lines of 'I must admit I don't have the faintest idea of what is going on.' Sunny had now said this particular thing three times over the course of her life, and she was beginning to wonder if this was something she was only going to say more and more as she grew older.

'The last time you said that,' Klaus said with a smile, 'the three of us were trying to figure out the pages the Quagmires left behind.' He held out a page for Sunny to see, and then pointed to the words 'Ana Gram.'

'We thought this was someone's name,' Klaus said, 'but it's really a kind of code. An anagram is when you move the letters around in one or more words to make another word or words.'

'Still pietrisycamollaviadelrechiote-mexity,' Sunny said with a sigh.

'I'll give you an example,' Klaus said. 'It's the example the Quagmires found. Look, on the same page they wrote "Al Funcoot." That's the name of the man who wrote *The Marvelous Marriage*, that dreadful play Count Olaf forced us to participate in.'

142

'Yuck,' Sunny said, which meant 'Don't remind me.'

'But look,' Klaus said. ' "Al Funcoot" has all the same letters as "Count Olaf." Olaf just rearranged the letters in his name to hide the fact that he really wrote the play himself. You see?'

'Phromein,' Sunny said, which meant something like 'I think I understand, but it's difficult for someone as young as myself.'

'It's difficult for me, too,' Klaus said. 'That's why the alphabet soup will come in handy. Count Olaf uses anagrams when he wants to hide something, and right now he's hiding our sister. I bet she's somewhere on this list, but her name's been scrambled up. The soup is going to help unscramble her.'

'But how?' Sunny asked.

'It's difficult to figure out anagrams if you can't move the letters around,' Klaus said. 'Normally, alphabet blocks or lettered tiles would be perfect, but alphabet noodles will do in a pinch. Now, hurry and open a can of soup.'

Sunny grinned, showing all of her

143

sharp, sharp teeth, and then swung her head down onto the can of soup, remembering the day she had learned to open cans all by herself. It was not that long ago, although it felt like it was in the very distant past, because it was before the Baudelaire mansion burned down, when the entire family was happy and together. It was the Baudelaires' mother's birthday, and she was sleeping late while everyone baked a cake for her. Violet was beating the eggs, butter, and sugar with a mixing device she had invented herself. Klaus was sifting the flour with the cinnamon, pausing every few minutes to wipe his glasses. And the Baudelaires' father was making his famous cream-cheese frosting, which would be spread thickly on top of the cake. All was going well until the electric can opener broke, and Violet didn't have the proper tools to fix it. The Baudelaires' father desperately needed to open a can of condensed milk to make his frosting, and for a moment it looked like the cake was going to be ruined. But Sunny—who

144

had been playing quietly on the floor this whole time—said her first word, 'Bite,' and bit down on the can, poking four small holes so the sweet, thick milk could pour out. The Baudelaires laughed and applauded, and the children's mother came downstairs, and from then on they used Sunny whenever they needed to open a can of anything, except for beets. Now, as the youngest Baudelaire bit along the edge of the can of alphabet soup, she wondered if one of her parents had really survived the fire, and if she dared get her hopes up just because of one sentence on page thirteen of the Snicket file. Sunny wondered if the Baudelaire family would ever be together again, laughing and clapping and working together to make something sweet and delicious.

'All done,' Sunny said finally.

'Good work, Sunny,' Klaus said. 'Now, let's try to find alphabet noodles that spell Violet's name.

'V?' Sunny asked.

'That's right,' Klaus said. 'V-I-O-L-E-T-B-A-U-D-E-L-A-I-R-E.'

The two younger Baudelaires reached into the can of soup and sorted through the diced carrots, chopped celery, blanched potatoes, roasted peppers, and steamed peas, which were all in a rich and creamy broth made from a secret blend of herbs and spices, to find the noodles they needed. The soup was cold from sitting in the closet for months and months, and occasionally they would find the right letter only to have it fall into pieces, or slip from their clammy fingers back into the can, but before too long they had found a V, an I, an O, an L, an E, a T, a B, an A, a U, a D, another E, another L, another A, another I, an R, and a bit of carrot they decided to use when a third E was not to be found.

'Now,' Klaus said, after they laid all of the noodles on top of another can so they could move them around. 'Let's take another look at the list of patients. Mattathias announced that the operation would take place in the Surgical Ward, so let's look in that section of the list, and try to see if any names look like good bets.'

Sunny poured the rest of soup into the sink and nodded in agreement, and Klaus hurriedly found the Surgical Ward section of the list and read the names of the patients:

LISA N. LOOTNDAY
ALBERT E. DEVILOEIA
LINDA RHALDEEN
ADA O. UBERVILLET
ED VALIANTBRUE
LAURA V. BLEEDIOTIE
MONTY KENSICLE
NED H. RIRGER
ERIQ BLUTHETTS
RUTH DERCROUMP
AL BRISNOW
CARRIE E. ABELABUDITE

'Goodness!' Klaus said. 'Every single patient on the list has a name that looks like an anagram. How in the world can we sort through all these names before it's too late?'

'V!' Sunny said.

'You're right,' Klaus said. 'Any name that doesn't have a V in it can't be an anagram of "Violet Baudelaire." We could cross those off the list—if we had a pen, that is.'

Sunny reached thoughtfully into one of the white medical coats, wondering what doctors might keep in their pockets. She found a surgical mask, which is perfect for covering one's face, and a pair of rubber gloves, that are perfect for protecting one's hands, and at the very bottom of the pocket she found a ballpoint pen, which is perfect for crossing out names which aren't the anagrams you're looking for. With a grin, Sunny handed the pen to Klaus, who quickly crossed out the names without Vs. Now the list looked like this:

~~LISA N. LOOTNDAY~~
ALBERT E. DEVILOEIA
~~LINDA RHALDEEN~~
ADA O. UBERVILLET
ED VALIANTBRUE
LAURA V. BLEEDIOTIE
~~MONTY KENSICLE~~
~~NED H. RIRCER~~
~~ERIQ BLUTHETTS~~

'That makes it much easier,' Klaus said. 'Now, let's move around the letters in Violet's name and see if we can spell out "Albert E. Deviloeia."'

Working carefully to avoid breaking them, Klaus began to move the noodles he and Sunny had taken out of the soup, and soon learned that "Albert E. Deviloeia" and 'Violet Baudelaire' were not quite anagrams. They were close, but they did not have the exact same letters in their names.

'Albert E. Deviloeia must be an actual sick person,' Klaus said in disappointment. 'Let's try to spell out "Ada O. Ubervillet."'

Once again, the supply closet was filled with the sound of shifting noodles, a faint and damp sound that made the children think of something slimy emerging from a swamp. It was, however, a far nicer sound than the one that interrupted their anagram decoding.

'Attention! Attention!' Mattathias's

149

voice sounded particularly snide as it called for attention from the square speaker over the Baudelaires' heads. 'The Surgical Ward will now be closed for the cranioectomy. Only Dr. Flacutono and his associates will be allowed into the ward until the patient is dead—I mean, until the operation is over. That is all.'

'Velocity!' Sunny shrieked.

'I *know* we have to hurry!' Klaus cried. 'I'm moving these noodles as quickly as I can! Ada O. Ubervillet isn't right, either!' He turned to the list of patients again to see who was next, and accidentally hit a noodle with his elbow, knocking it to the floor with a moist *splat*. Sunny picked it up for him, but the fall had split it into two pieces. Instead of an O, the Baudelaires now had a pair of parentheses.

'That's O.K.,' Klaus said hurriedly. 'The next name on the list is Ed Valiantbrue, which doesn't have an O in it anyway.'

'O!' Sunny shrieked.

'O!' Klaus agreed.

'O!' Sunny insisted.

'Oh!' Klaus cried. 'I see what you mean! If it doesn't have an O in it, it can't be an anagram of Violet Baudelaire. That only leaves one name on the list: Laura V. Bleediotie. That must be the one we're looking for.'

'Check!' Sunny said, and held her breath as Klaus moved the noodles around. In a few seconds, the name of the eldest Baudelaire sister had been transformed into Laura V. Bleediotie, except for the O, which Sunny still held in pieces in her tiny fist, and the last E, which was still a piece of carrot.

'It's her, all right,' Klaus said, with a grin of triumph. 'We've found Violet.'

'Asklu,' Sunny said, which meant 'We never would have found her if you hadn't figured out that Olaf was using anagrams.'

'It was really the Quagmire triplets who figured it out,' Klaus said, holding up the notebook page, 'and it was you who opened the cans of soup, which made it much easier. But before we congratulate ourselves, let's rescue our sister.' Klaus took a look at the list of patients. 'We'll find "Laura V.

Bleediotie" in Room 922 of the Surgical Ward.'

'Gwito,' Sunny pointed out, which meant 'But Mattathias closed the Surgical Ward.'

'Then we'll have to open it,' Klaus said grimly, and took a good look around the supply closet. 'Let's put on those white medical coats,' he said. 'Maybe if we look like doctors, we can get into the ward. We can use these surgical masks in the pocket to hide our faces—just like Olaf's associate did at the lumbermill.'

'Quagmire,' Sunny said doubtfully, which meant 'When the Quagmires used disguises, they didn't fool Olaf.'

'But when Olaf used disguises,' Klaus said, 'he fooled everyone.'

'Us,' Sunny said.

'Except us,' Klaus agreed, 'but we don't have to fool ourselves.'

'True,' Sunny said, and reached for two white coats. Because most doctors are adults, the white coats were far too big for the children, who were reminded of the enormous pinstripe suits Esmé Squalor had purchased for them when she had been their guardian. Klaus helped Sunny roll up the sleeves of her coat, and Sunny helped Klaus tie his mask around his face, and in a few moments the children were finished putting on their disguises.

'Let's go,' Klaus said, and put his hand on the door of the supply closet. But he did not open it. Instead he turned back to his sister, and the two Baudelaires looked at each other. Even though the siblings were wearing white coats, and had surgical masks on their faces, they did not look like doctors. They looked like two children in white coats with surgical masks on their faces. Their disguises looked spurious —a word which here means 'nothing at all like a real doctor'—and yet they were no more spurious than the disguises that Olaf had been using since his first attempt to steal the Baudelaire fortune. Klaus and Sunny looked at one another and hoped that Olaf's methods would work for them, and help them steal their sister, and without another word, they opened the door and stepped out of the supply closet.

'Douth?' Sunny asked, which meant 'But how are we going to find the Surgical Ward, when the maps of this hospital are so confusing?'

'We'll have to find someone who is going there,' Klaus said. 'Look for somebody who looks like they're on their way to the Surgical Ward.'

'Silata,' Sunny said. She meant something along the lines of 'But there are so many people here,' and she was right. Although the Volunteers Fighting Disease were nowhere to be seen, the hallways of Heimlich Hospital were full of people. A hospital needs many different people and many different types of equipment in order to work properly, and as Klaus and Sunny tried to find the Surgical Ward they saw all sorts of hospital employees and devices hurrying through the halls. There were physicians carrying stethoscopes, hurrying to listen to people's heartbeats, and there were obstetricians carrying babies, hurrying to deliver people's children. There were radiologists carrying X-ray machines, hurrying to view people's insides, and there were optic surgeons carrying laser-driven technology, hurrying to get inside people's views. There were nurses carrying hypodermic needles, hurrying to give people shots, and there were administrators carrying clipboards, hurrying to catch up on important paperwork. But no matter where the Baudelaires looked, they couldn't see anyone who seemed to be hurrying to the Surgical Ward.

'I don't see any surgeons,' Klaus said in desperation.

'Peipix,' Sunny said, which meant 'Me neither.'

'Out of my way, everybody!' demanded a voice at the end of the hallway. 'I'm a surgical assistant, carrying equipment for Dr. Flacutono!'

The other employees of the hospital stopped and cleared the way for the person who had spoken, a tall person dressed in a white lab coat and a surgical mask who was coming down the hallway in odd, tottering steps.

'I've got to get to the Surgical Ward

155

right away!' the person called, walking past the Baudelaires without even glancing at them. But Klaus and Sunny glanced at this person. They saw, beneath the bottom hem of the white coat, the pair of shoes with stiletto heels that this person was wearing, and they saw the handbag in the shape of an eye that the person was holding in one hand. The children saw the black veil of the person's hat, which was hanging in front of the surgical mask, and they saw blotches of lipstick, which had soaked through from the person's lips and were staining the bottom of the mask.

The person, of course, was pretending to be a surgical assistant, and she was carrying something that was pretending to be a piece of surgical equipment, but the children did not need more than a glance to see through both of these spurious disguises. As they watched the person tottering down the hallway, the two Baudelaires knew at once that she was really Esmé Squalor, the villainous girlfriend of Count Olaf. And as they looked at the thing she was carrying, glinting in the light of the hospital hallway, the two Baudelaires knew that it was nothing more than a large rusty knife, with a long row of jagged teeth, just perfect for a cranioectomy.

CHAPTER TEN

At this point in the dreadful story I am writing, I must interrupt for a moment and describe something that happened to a good friend of mine named Mr. Sirin. Mr. Sirin was a lepidopterist, a word which usually means 'a person who studies butterflies.'

In this case, however, the word 'lepidopterist' means 'a man who was

being pursued by angry government officials,' and on the night I am telling you about they were right on his heels. Mr. Sirin looked back to see how close they were—four officers in their bright-pink uniforms, with small flashlights in their left hands and large nets in their right—and realized that in a moment they would catch up, and arrest him and his six favorite butterflies, which were frantically flapping alongside him. Mr. Sirin did not care much if he was captured—he had been in prison four and a half times over the course of his long and complicated life—but he cared very much about the butterflies. He realized that these six delicate insects would undoubtedly perish in bug prison, where poisonous spiders, stinging bees, and other criminals would rip them to shreds. So, as the secret police closed in, Mr. Sirin opened his mouth as wide as he could and swallowed all six butterflies whole, quickly placing them in the dark but safe confines of his empty stomach. It was not a pleasant feeling to have these six insects living inside him, but

Mr. Sirin kept them there for three years, eating only the lightest foods served in prison so as not to crush the insects with a clump of broccoli or a baked potato. When his prison sentence was over, Mr. Sirin burped up the grateful butterflies and resumed his lepidoptery work in a community that was much more friendly to scientists and their specimens.

I am telling you this story not just to reveal the courage and imagination of one of my dearest friends, but to help you imagine how Klaus and Sunny felt as they watched Esmé Squalor, disguised as an associate of Dr. Flacutono, walk down the hallway of Heimlich Hospital carrying the long, rusty knife disguised as a surgical tool to be used on Violet. The two youngsters realized that their only chance of finding the Surgical Ward and rescuing their sister was to try and fool this greedy and stiletto-heeled villain, but as they approached her, like Mr. Sirin during his fifth and final prison sentence, the two Baudelaires felt the unpleasant fluttering of butterflies in their stomachs.

'Excuse me, ma'am,' Klaus said, trying to sound less like a thirteen-year-old boy and more like someone who had graduated from medical school. 'Did you say you were an associate of Dr. Flacutono?'

'If you're someone with a hearing problem,' Esmé said rudely, 'don't bother me. Go to the Ear Ward.'

'I'm not someone with a hearing problem,' Klaus said. 'This woman and I are associates of Dr. Flacutono.'

Esmé stopped in the middle of stabbing the floor, and stared down at the two siblings. Klaus and Sunny could see her eyes shining behind the veil of her fashionable hat as she regarded the children before replying.

'I was just wondering where you were,' she said. 'Come along with me, and I'll take you to the patient.'

'Patsy,' Sunny said.

'What she is saying,' Klaus said quickly, 'is that we're very concerned about Laura V. Bleediotie.'

'Well, you won't be concerned for long,' Esmé replied, leading the children around a corner to another hallway. 'Here, you carry the knife.'

The evil girlfriend handed Klaus the rusty blade, and leaned in closely to talk with him. 'I'm glad you two are here,' she whispered. 'The brat's little brother and sister haven't been captured yet, and we still don't have the file on the Snicket fires. The authorities removed it for their investigation. The boss says we might have to torch the place.'

'Torch?' Sunny asked.

'Mattathias will take care of that part,' Esmé said, looking around the hallway to make sure no one could hear them. 'All you have to do is assist with the surgery. Let's hurry up.'

Esmé walked up a stairway as fast as her shoes could carry her, and the children followed nervously behind her, Klaus holding the rusty, jagged knife. With every door they opened, every hallway they walked down, and every staircase they ascended, the youngsters were afraid that at any moment Esmé would see through their disguises and realize who they were.

But the greedy woman was too busy pausing to yank the blades of the stiletto heels out of the floor to notice that the two additional associates of Dr. Flacutono bore a very strong resemblance to the children she was trying to capture. Finally, Esmé led the Baudelaires to a door marked 'Surgical Ward,' which was being guarded by someone the children recognized at once. The guard was wearing a coat which read 'Heimlich Hospital' and a cap that had the word 'GUARD' printed on it in big black print, but Klaus and Sunny could see that this was another spurious disguise. The siblings had seen this person at Damocles Dock, when poor Aunt Josephine had been their guardian, and they'd had to cook for this person when they'd been living with Count Olaf. The spurious guard was an enormous person who looked like neither a man nor a woman, and who had been assisting Count Olaf with his nefarious schemes for as long as the Baudelaires had been escaping from them. The person looked at the children, and the

163

children look back at him or her, certain that they would be recognized. But Olaf's assistant merely nodded and opened the door.

'They've already anesthetized the bratty orphan,' Esmé said, 'so you ladies merely need to go to her room and bring her to the operating theater. I'm going to try to find that sniveling bookworm and that stupid baby with the over-sized teeth. Mattathias says I get to choose which one to keep alive in order to force Mr. Poe to give us the fortune, and which one I get to rip to shreds.'

'Good,' Klaus said, trying to sound fierce and villainous. 'I'm so tired of chasing those kids around.'

'Me, too,' Esmé said, and the enormous assistant nodded in agreement. 'But I'm sure this will be the last time. Once we've destroyed the file, nobody can accuse us of any crimes, and once we murder the orphans, the fortune will be ours.'

The villainous woman paused and looked around her to make sure no one was listening, and then, satisfied that no one could hear her, she laughed wildly in triumph. The enormous assistant laughed, too, an odd laugh that sounded like a squeal and a howl at the same time, and the two Baudelaire youngsters tilted back their masked faces and made noises as if they were laughing, too, although their laughter was as spurious as their disguises. Klaus and Sunny felt more like being sick than laughing as they pretended to be as greedy and evil as Count Olaf and his troupe. It had never occurred to the children how these terrible people acted when they didn't have to pretend to be nice, and the two siblings were horrified to hear all the bloodthirsty things Esmé had said. Watching Esmé and the enormous assistant laugh together made the butterflies in the Baudelaire stomachs flutter all the more, and the youngsters were relieved when Esmé finally stopped laughing, and ushered the children into the Surgical Ward.

'I'll leave you ladies in the hands of our associates,' she said, and the Baudelaires immediately saw with horror what she meant. Esmé shut the door behind them, and the children found themselves facing two more of Count Olaf's wicked associates.

'Well, hello there,' the first one said in a sinister voice, pointing at the two children with an odd-looking hand. One of the fingers was curved at an odd angle while the others hung limp, like socks hung out to dry, and Klaus and Sunny could see at once that this was the associate of Olaf who had hooks instead of hands, wearing rubber gloves to hide his unusual and dangerous appendages. Behind him was a man whose hands were not as familiar, but Klaus and Sunny recognized him just as easily, due to the hideous wig he was wearing on his head. The wig was so limp, white, and curly that it looked like a heap of dead worms, which is not the sort of wig one forgets. The children had certainly not forgotten it from when they had been living in Paltryville, and realized at once that this person was the bald man with the long nose who had been assisting Count Olaf since the

Baudelaires' troubles began. The hook-handed man and the bald man with the long nose were among the nastiest members of Olaf's troupe, but unlike the majority of nasty people of this earth, they were also quite clever, and the two young siblings felt the butterfly feeling in their stomachs increase exponentially—a phrase which here means 'get much, much worse'— as they waited to see if these two associates were clever enough to see through the children's disguises.

'I can see through your disguise,' the hook-handed man continued, and placed one of his spurious hands on Klaus's shoulder.

'Me, too,' the bald man said, 'but I don't think anyone else will. I don't know how you ladies managed to do it, but you look much shorter in those white coats.'

'And your faces don't look as pale in those surgical masks,' the hook-handed man agreed. 'These are the best disguises Olaf—I mean *Mattathias*— has ever cooked up.'

'We don't have time for all this

talking,' Klaus said, hoping that the associates wouldn't recognize his voice, either. 'We've got to get to Room 922 right away.'

'You're right, of course,' the hook-handed man said. 'Follow us.'

The two associates began walking down the hallway of the Surgical Ward as Klaus and Sunny looked at one another in relief.

'Gwit,' Sunny murmured, which meant 'They didn't recognize us either.'

'I know,' Klaus replied in a whisper. 'They think we're the two powder-faced women, disguised as associates of Dr. Flacutono, instead of two children disguised as the two powder-faced women disguised as associates of Dr. Flacutono.'

'Stop all that whispering about disguises,' the bald man said. 'If anyone hears you, it'll be the end of us.'

'Instead of the end of Laura V. Bleediotie,' the hook-handed man said with a sneer. 'I've been waiting to get hooks on her since she escaped from marrying Mattathias.'

168

'Trapped,' Sunny said, sneering as best she could.

'Trapped is right,' the bald man said. 'I al-ready gave her the anesthetic, so she's unconscious. All we have to do is lead her to the operating theater, and you can saw her head off.'

'I still don't understand why we have to murder her in front of all those doctors,' the hook-handed man said.

'So it can look like an accident, you idiot,' the bald man snarled in reply.

'I'm not an idiot,' the hook-handed man said, stopping to glare at his fellow associate. 'I'm physically handicapped.'

'Just because you're physically handicapped doesn't mean you're mentally clever,' the bald man said.

'And just because you're wearing an ugly wig,' the hook-handed man said, 'doesn't mean you can insult me.'

'Stop all this arguing!' Klaus said. 'The sooner we can operate on Laura V. Bleediotie, the sooner we'll all be rich.'

'Yes!' Sunny said.

The two criminals looked down at the Baudelaires, and then nodded at

169

one another sheepishly. 'The ladies are right,' the hook-handed man said. 'We shouldn't behave unprofessionally, just because it's been a very stressful time at work.'

'I know,' the bald man said with a sigh. 'It seems like we've been following these three orphans forever, only to have them slip out of our grasp at the last minute. Let's just focus on getting the job done, and work out our personal problems later. Well, here we are.'

The four disguised people had reached the end of a hallway and were standing in front of a door marked 'Room 922,' with the name 'Laura V. Bleediotie' scrawled on a piece of paper and taped beneath. The bald man took a key out of the pocket in his medical coat, and unlocked the door with a triumphant grin. 'Here she is,' he said. 'Our little sleeping beauty.'

The door opened with a long, whiny creak, and the children stepped inside the room, which was square and small and had heavy shades over the windows, making it quite dark inside.

But even in the dim light the children could see their sister, and they almost gasped at how dreadful she looked.

When the bald associate had mentioned a sleeping beauty, he was referring to a fairy tale that you have probably heard one thousand times. Like all fairy tales, the story of Sleeping Beauty begins with 'Once upon a time,' and continues with a foolish young princess who makes a witch very angry, and then takes a nap until her boyfriend wakes her up with a kiss and insists on getting married, at which point the story ends with the phrase 'happily ever after.' The story is usually illustrated with fancy drawings of the napping princess, who always looks very glamorous and elegant, with her hair neatly combed and a long silk gown keeping her comfortable as she snores away for years and years. But when Klaus and Sunny saw Violet in Room 922, it looked nothing like a fairy tale.

The eldest Baudelaire was lying on a gurney, which is a metal bed with wheels, used in hospitals to move patients around. This particular gurney was as rusty as the knife Klaus was holding, and its sheets were ripped and soiled. Olaf's associates had put her into a white gown as filthy as the sheets, and had twisted her legs together like vines. Her hair had been messily thrown over her eyes so that no one would recognize her face from *The Daily Punctilio*, and her arms hung loosely from her body, one of them almost touching the floor of the room with one limp finger. Her face was pale, as pale and empty as the surface of the moon, and her mouth was open slightly in a vacant frown, as if she were dreaming of being pricked with a pin. Violet looked like she had dropped onto the gurney from a great height, and if it were not for the slow and steady rise of her chest as she breathed, it would have looked like she had not survived the fall. Klaus and Sunny looked at her in horrified silence, trying not to cry as they gazed at their helpless sister.

'She's a pretty one,' the hook-handed man said, 'even when

she's unconscious.'

'She's clever, too,' the bald man said, 'although her clever little brain won't do her any good when her head has been sawed off.'

'Let's hurry up and go to the operating theater,' the hook-handed man said, beginning to move the gurney out of the room. 'Mattathias said the anesthetic would last for only a little while, so we'd best start the cranioectomy.'

'I wouldn't mind if she woke up in the middle of it,' the bald man said with a giggle, 'but I suppose that would ruin the plan. You ladies take the head end. I don't like to look at her when she's frowning like that.'

'And don't forget the knife,' the hook-handed man said. 'Dr. Flacutono and I will be supervising, but you two will actually perform the operation.'

The two children nodded, afraid that if they tried to speak, the two henchmen would hear how anxious they were and become suspicious. In silence they took their places at the gurney where their sister lay without moving. The Baudelaires wanted to gently shake her by the shoulders, or whisper in her ear, or even just brush the hair away from her eyes—anything at all to help their unconscious sibling. But the two youngsters knew that any affectionate gesture would give away their disguise, so they just walked alongside the gurney, clutching the rusty knife, as the two men led the way out of Room 922 and through the halls of the Surgical Ward. With every step, Klaus and Sunny watched their sister carefully, hoping for a sign that the anesthesia was wearing off, but Violet's face remained as still and blank as the sheet of paper on which I am printing this story.

Although her siblings preferred to think about her inventing abilities and conversational skills rather than her physical appearance, it was true, as the hook-handed man had said, that Violet was a pretty one, and if her hair had been neatly combed, instead of all tangled up, and she had been dressed in something elegant and glamorous, instead of a stained gown, she might indeed have looked like an illustration from 'Sleeping Beauty.' But the two younger Baudelaires did not feel like characters in a fairy tale. The unfortunate events in their lives had not begun with 'Once upon a time,' but with the terrible fire that had destroyed their home, and as Olaf's associates led them to a square metal door at the end of the hallway, Klaus and Sunny feared that their lives would not end like a fairy tale either. The label on the door read 'Operating Theater,' and as the hook-handed man opened it with one curved glove, the two children could not imagine that their story would end with 'happily ever after.'

CHAPTER ELEVEN

Operating theaters are not nearly as popular as dramatic theaters, musical theaters, and movie theaters, and it is easy to see why. A dramatic theater is a large, dark room in which actors perform a play, and if you are in the audience, you can enjoy yourself by listening to the dialog and looking at the costumes. A musical theater is a large, dark room in which musicians perform a symphony, and if you are in the audience, you can enjoy yourself

by listening to the melodies and watching the conductor wave his little stick around. And a movie theater is a large, dark room in which a projectionist shows a film, and if you are in the audience, you can enjoy yourself by eating popcorn and gossiping about movie stars. But an operating theater is a large, dark room in which doctors perform medical procedures, and if you are in the audience, the best thing to do is to leave at once, because there is never anything on display in an operating theater but pain, suffering, and discomfort, and for this reason most operating theaters have been closed down or have been turned into restaurants.

I'm sorry to say, however, that the operating theater at Heimlich Hospital was still quite popular at the time this story takes place. As Klaus and Sunny followed Olaf's two disguised associates through the square metal door, they saw that the large, dark room was filled with people. There were rows of doctors in white coats who were clearly eager to see a new operation being performed. There were clusters of nurses sitting together and whispering with excitement about the world's first cranioectomy. There was a large group of Volunteers Fighting Disease who seemed ready to burst into song if needed. And there were a great many people who looked like they had simply walked over to the operating theater to see what was playing. The four disguised people wheeled the gurney onto a small bare stage, lit by a chandelier that was hanging from the ceiling, and as soon as the light of the chandelier fell on Klaus and Sunny's unconscious sister, all of the audience members burst into cheers and applause. The roar from the crowd only made Klaus and Sunny even more anxious, but Olaf's two associates stopped moving the gurney, raised their arms, and bowed several times.

'Thank you very much!' the hook-handed man cried. 'Doctors, nurses, Volunteers Fighting Disease, reporters from *The Daily Punctilio*, distinguished

178

guests, and regular people, welcome to the operating theater at Heimlich Hospital. I am Dr. O. Lucafont, and I will be your medical host for today's performance.'

'Hooray for Dr. Lucafont!' a doctor cried, as the crowd burst into applause again, and the hook-handed man raised his rubber-gloved hands and took another bow.

'And I am Dr. Flacutono,' the bald man announced, looking a bit jealous of all the applause the hook-handed man was getting. 'I am the surgeon who invented the cranioectomy, and I am thrilled to operate today in front of all you wonderful and attractive people.'

'Hooray for Dr. Flacutono!' a nurse shouted, and the crowd applauded again. Some of the reporters even whistled as the bald man bowed deeply, using one hand to hold his curly wig on his head.

'The surgeon is right!' the hook-handed man said. 'You are wonderful and attractive, all of you! Go on, give yourselves a big hand!'

'Hooray for us!' a volunteer cried,

and the audience applauded another time. The two Baudelaires looked at their older sister, hoping that the noise of the crowd would wake her up, but Violet did not move.

'Now, the two lovely ladies you see are two associates of mine named Dr. Tocuna and Nurse Flo,' the bald man continued. 'Why don't you give them the same wonderful welcome you gave us?'

Klaus and Sunny half expected someone in the crowd to shout, 'They aren't medical associates! They're those two children wanted for murder!' but instead the crowd merely cheered once more, and the two children found themselves waving miserably at the members of the audience. Although the youngsters were relieved that they hadn't been recognized, the butterflies in their stomachs only got worse as everyone in the operating theater grew more and more eager for the operation to begin.

'And now that you've met all of our fantastic performers,' the hook-handed man said, 'let the show begin. Dr.

Flacutono, are you ready to begin?'

'I sure am,' the bald man said. 'Now, ladies and gentlemen, as I'm sure you know, a cranioectomy is a procedure in which the patient's head is removed. Scientists have discovered that many health problems are rooted in the brain, so that the best thing to do with a sick patient is remove it. However, a cranioectomy is as dangerous as it is necessary. There is a chance that Laura V. Bleediotie might die while the operation is being performed, but sometimes one must risk accidents in order to cure illness.'

'A patient's death would certainly be a terrible accident, Dr. Flacutono,' the hook-handed man said.

'It sure would, Dr. O. Lucafont,' the bald man agreed. 'That's why I'm going to have my associates perform the surgery, while I supervise. Dr. Tocuna and Nurse Flo, you may begin.'

The crowd applauded once more, and Olaf's associates bowed and blew kisses to each corner of the operating theater as the two children looked at one another in horror.

'What can we do?' Klaus murmured to his sister, looking out at the crowd. 'We're surrounded by people who expect us to saw Violet's head off.'

Sunny looked at Violet, still unconscious on the gurney, and then at her brother, who was holding the long, rusty knife Esmé had given him. 'Stall,' she said. The word 'stall' has two meanings, but as with most words with two meanings, you can figure out which meaning is being used by looking at the situation. The word 'stall,' for example, can refer to a place where horses are kept, but Klaus knew at once that Sunny meant something more along the lines of 'We'll try to postpone the operation as long as we can, Klaus,' and he nodded silently in agreement. The middle Baudelaire took a deep breath and closed his eyes, trying to think of something that could help him postpone the cranioectomy, and all at once he thought of something he had read.

When you read as many books as Klaus Baudelaire, you are going to learn a great deal of information that might not become useful for a long time. You might read a book that would teach you all about the exploration of outer space, even if you do not become an astronaut until you are eighty years old. You might read a book about how to perform tricks on ice skates, and then not be forced to perform these tricks for a few weeks. You might read a book on how to have a successful marriage, when the only woman you will ever love has married someone else and then perished one terrible afternoon. But although Klaus had read books on outer-space exploration, ice-skating tricks, and good marriage methods, and not yet found much use for this information, he had learned a great deal of information that was about to become very useful indeed.

'Before I make the first incision,' Klaus said, using a fancy word for 'cut' in order to sound more like a medical professional, 'I think Nurse Flo and I should talk a little bit about the equipment we're using.'

Sunny looked at her brother

quizzically. 'Knife?' she asked.

'That's right,' Klaus said. 'It's a knife, and—'

'We all know it's a knife, Dr. Tocuna,' the hook-handed man said, smiling at the audience, as the bald man leaned in to whisper to Klaus.

'What are you doing?' he hissed. 'Just saw off the brat's head and we'll be done.'

'A real doctor would never perform a new operation without explaining everything,' Klaus whispered back. 'We have to keep talking, or we'll never fool them.'

Olaf's associates looked at Klaus and Sunny for a moment, and the two Baudelaires got ready to run, dragging Violet's gurney with them, if they were recognized at last. But after a moment's hesitation, the two disguised men looked at each other and nodded.

'I suppose you're right,' the hook-handed man said, and then turned to the audience. 'Sorry for the delay, folks. As you know, we're real doctors, so that's why we're explaining everything. Carry on, Dr. Tocuna.'

'The cranioectomy will be performed with a knife,' Klaus said, 'which is the oldest surgical tool in the world.' He was remembering the section on knives in *A Complete History of Surgical Tools*, which he had read when he was eleven. 'Early knives have been found in Egyptian tombs and Mayan temples, where they were used for ceremonial purposes, and mostly fashioned out of stone. Gradually bronze and iron became the essential materials in knives, although some cultures fashioned them out of the incisors of slain animals.'

'Teeth,' Sunny explained.

'There are a number of different types of knives,' Klaus continued, 'including the pocket-knife, the penknife, and the drawing knife, but the one required for this cranioectomy is a Bowie knife, named after Colonel James Bowie, who lived in Texas.'

'Wasn't that a magnificient explanation, ladies and gentlemen?' the hook-handed man said.

'It sure was,' one of the reporters agreed. She was a woman wearing a gray suit and chewing gum as she spoke into a small microphone. 'I can see the headline now: "DOCTOR AND NURSE EXPLAIN HISTORY OF KNIFE." Wait until the readers of *The Daily Punctilio* see that!'

The audience applauded in agreement, and as the operating theater filled with the sound of cheers and clapping, Violet moved on her gurney, ever so slightly. Her mouth opened a little wider, and one of her limp hands stirred briefly. The motions were so small that only Klaus and Sunny noticed them, and they looked at one another hopefully. Could they keep stalling until the anesthesia completely wore off?

'Enough talk,' the bald man whispered to the children. 'It's lots of fun fooling innocent people, but we'd better get on with the operation before the orphan wakes up.'

'Before I make the first incision,' Klaus said again, continuing to address the audience as if the bald man hadn't spoken, 'I would like to say a few words concerning rust.' He paused for a

186

moment and tried to remember what he had learned from a book entitled *What Happens to Wet Metal*, which he had received as a gift from his mother. 'Rust is a reddish-brown coating that forms on certain metals when they oxidize, which is a scientific term for a chemical reaction occurring when iron or steel comes into contact with moisture.' He held up the rusty knife for the audience to see, and out of the corner of his eye, he saw Violet's hand move again, just barely. 'The oxidation process is integral to a cranioectomy due to the oxidative processes of cellular mitochondria and cosmetic demystification,' he continued, trying to use as many complicated words as he could think of.

'Clap!' Sunny cried, and the audience applauded once more, although not as loudly this time.

'Very impressive,' the bald associate said, glaring at Klaus over his surgical mask. 'But I think these lovely people will understand the process better once the head has actually been removed.'

'Of course,' Klaus replied. 'But first,

we need to tenderize the vertebrae, so we can make a clean cut. Nurse Flo, will you please nibble on Viol—I mean, on Laura V. Bleediotie's neck?'

'Yes,' Sunny said with a smile, knowing just what Klaus was up to. Standing on tiptoe, the youngest Baudelaire gave her sister a few small nibbles on the neck, hoping that it would wake Violet up. As Sunny's teeth scraped against her skin, Violet twitched, and shut her mouth, but nothing more.

'What are you doing?' the hook-handed man demanded in a furious whisper. 'Perform the operation at once, or Mattathias will be furious!'

'Isn't Nurse Flo wonderful?' Klaus asked the audience, but only a few members of the crowd clapped, and there was not a single cheer. The people in the operating theater were clearly eager to see some surgery rather than hear any more explanations.

'I believe you've bitten her neck enough,' the bald man said. His voice was friendly and professional, but his

188

eyes were gazing at the children suspiciously. 'Let's get on with the cranioectomy.'

Klaus nodded, and clasped the knife in both hands, holding it up over his helpless sister. He looked at Violet's sleeping figure and wondered if he could made a very small cut on Violet's neck, one that could wake her up but wouldn't injure her. He looked at the rusty blade, which was shaking up and down as his hands trembled in fear. And then he looked at Sunny, who had stopped nibbling on Violet's neck and was looking up at him with wide, wide eyes.

'I can't do it,' he whispered, and looked up at the ceiling. High above them was a square intercom speaker that he had not noticed before, and the sight of the speaker made him think of something. 'I can't do it,' he announced, and there was a gasp from the crowd.

The hook-handed man took a step toward the gurney, and pointed his limp, curved glove at Klaus. The middle Baudelaire could see the sharp tip of his hook, poking through the finger of the glove like a sea creature emerging from the water. 'Why not?' the hook-handed man asked quietly.

Klaus swallowed, hoping he still sounded like a medical professional instead of a scared child. 'Before I make the first incision, there's one more thing that has to be done—the most important thing we do here at Heimlich Hospital.'

'And what is that?' the bald man asked. His surgical mask curled down as he gave the children a sinister frown, but Sunny's mask began to curl in the opposite direction as she realized what Klaus was talking about, and began to smile.

'Paperwork!' she said, and to the Baudelaires' delight, the audience began to applaud once more.

'Hooray!' called a member of V.F.D. from the back of the operating theater, as the cheering continued. 'Hooray for paperwork!'

Olaf's two associates looked at one another in frustration as the Baudelaires looked at one another in relief. 'Hooray for paperwork indeed!' Klaus cried. 'We can't operate on a patient until her file is absolutely complete!'

'I can't believe we forgot about it, even for a moment!' a nurse cried. 'Paperwork is the most important thing we do at this hospital!'

'I can see the headline now,' said the reporter who had spoken earlier. "HEIMLICH HOSPITAL ALMOST FORGETS PAPERWORK!" Wait until the readers of *The Daily Punctilio* see that!'

'Somebody call Hal,' suggested a doctor. 'He's in charge of the Library of Records, so he can solve this paperwork problem.'

'I'll call Hal right now!' announced a nurse, walking out of the operating theater, and the crowd clapped in support of her decision.

'There's no need to call Hal,' said the hook-handed man, holding up his hooked gloves to try to calm the crowd. 'The paperwork has been taken care of, I promise you.'

'But all surgical paperwork has to be

verified by Hal,' Klaus said. 'That's the policy of Heimlich Hospital.'

The bald man glared down at the children and spoke to them in a frightening whisper. 'What in the world are you doing?' he asked them. 'You're going to ruin everything!'

'I think Dr. Tocuna is right,' another doctor said. 'That's the policy here.'

The crowd applauded again, and Klaus and Sunny looked at one another. The two Baudelaires, of course, had no idea what the hospital's policy was concerning surgical paperwork, but they were beginning to see that the crowd would believe just about anything if they thought it was being said by a medical professional.

'Hal is on his way,' the nurse announced, re-entering the room. 'There's apparently been some problem at the Library of Records, but he'll come as quickly as he can and settle this matter once and for all.'

'We don't need Hal to settle this matter once and for all,' a voice said from the far end of the theater, and the Baudelaires turned to see the slender, tottering figure of Esmé Squalor, walking straight toward them in her stiletto-heeled shoes, with two people trailing dutifully behind her. These two people were both dressed in medical coats and surgical masks just like the Baudelaires'. Klaus and Sunny could see just a bit of their pale faces above the masks and knew at once that they were the two powder-faced assistants of Olaf.

'This is the *real* Dr. Tocuna,' Esmé said, pointing to one of the women, 'and *this* is the real Nurse Flo. The two people up on this stage are impostors.'

'No we're not,' the hook-handed man said angrily.

'Not you two,' Esmé said impatiently, glaring over her surgical mask at the two henchmen. 'I mean the other two people on the stage. They fooled everyone. They fooled doctors, nurses, volunteers, reporters, and even me—until I found the real associates of Dr. Flacutono, that is.'

'In my medical opinion,' Klaus said, 'I believe this woman has lost her mind.'

'I haven't lost my mind,' Esmé said with a snarl, 'but you're about to lose your heads, Baudelaires.'

'Baudelaires?' the reporter from *The Daily Punctilio* asked. 'The same Baudelaires who murdered Count Omar?'

'Olaf,' the bald man corrected.

'I'm confused,' whined a volunteer. 'There are too many people pretending to be other people.'

'Allow me to explain,' Esmé said, stepping up on the stage. 'I am a medical professional, just like Dr. Flacutono, Dr. O. Lucafont, Dr. Tocuna, and Nurse Flo. You can see that from our medical coats and surgical masks.'

'Us, too!' Sunny cried.

Esmé's surgical mask curled up in a wicked smile. 'Not for long,' she said, and in one swift gesture she ripped the masks off the Baudelaires' faces. The crowd gasped as the masks fluttered to the ground, and the two children saw the doctors, nurses, reporters, and regular people in the crowd look at them in horror. Only the Volunteers

Fighting Disease, who believed that no news was good news, did not recognize the youngsters.

'They *are* the Baudelaires!' a nurse exclaimed in astonishment. 'I read about them in *The Daily Punctilio*!'

'Me, too!' cried a doctor.

'It's always a pleasure to hear from our readers,' the reporter said modestly.

'But there were supposed to be *three* murderous orphans, not two!' another doctor said. 'Where's the oldest one?'

The hook-handed man hurriedly stepped in front of the gurney, shielding Violet from view. 'She's already in jail,' he said quickly.

'She is not!' Klaus said, and brushed Violet's hair out of her eyes so that everyone could see she was not Laura V. Bleediotie. 'These terrible people disguised her as a patient, so they could cut her head off!'

'Don't be ridiculous,' Esmé said. '*You're* the one who was trying to cut her head off. Look, you're still holding the knife.'

'That's true!' the reporter cried. 'I

can see the headline now: "MURDERER ATTEMPTS TO MURDER MURDERER." Wait until the readers of *The Daily Punctilio* see this!'

'Tweem!' Sunny shrieked.

'We're not murderers!' Klaus translated frantically.

'If you're not murderers,' the reporter said, holding out her microphone, 'then why have you sneaked into a hospital in disguise?'

'I think I can explain that,' said another familiar voice, and everyone turned to see Hal enter the operating theater. In one hand he was clutching the ring of keys the Baudelaires had made from paper clips and Violet's hair ribbon, and with the other hand he was pointing angrily at the children.

'Those three Baudelaire murderers,' he said, 'pretended to be volunteers in order to come to work in the Library of Records.'

'They did?' a nurse said, as the audience gasped. 'You mean they're murderers *and* phony volunteers?'

'No wonder they didn't know the words to the song!' a volunteer cried.

196

'Taking advantage of my poor eyesight,' Hal continued, pointing at his glasses, 'they made these fake keys and switched it with the real one, so they could sneak into the library and destroy the files about their crimes!'

'We didn't want to destroy the file,' Klaus said, 'we wanted to clear our names. I'm sorry we tricked you, Hal, and I'm sorry that some of the file cabinets were knocked over, but—'

'Knocked over?' Hal repeated. 'You did more than knock over cabinets.' He looked at the children and sighed wearily, and then turned to face the audience. 'These children committed arson,' he said. 'The Library of Records is burning as we speak.'

CHAPTER TWELVE

I am alone this evening, and I am alone because of a cruel twist of fate, a phrase which here means that nothing has happened the way I thought it would. Once I was a content man, with a comfortable home, a successful career, a person I loved very much, and an extremely reliable typewriter, but all of those things have been taken away

from me, and now the only trace I have of those happy days is the tattoo on my left ankle. As I sit in this very tiny room, printing these words with this very large pencil, I feel as if my whole life has been nothing but a dismal play, presented just for someone else's amusement, and that the playwright who invented my cruel twist of fate is somewhere far above me, laughing and laughing at his creation.

It is not pleasant to feel this way, and it is doubly unpleasant if the cruel twist of fate happens to you when you are actually standing on a stage and there is actually someone, far above you, laughing and laughing, as it was with the Baudelaire children in the operating theater of Heimlich Hospital. The children had scarcely heard Hal's accusation that they had burned down the Library of Records when they heard rough and familiar laughter coming out of the intercom speaker above them. The siblings had heard this laughter when Mattathias had first captured the Quagmire triplets, and when he had trapped the

Baudelaires in a locked Deluxe Cell. It was the triumphant laughter of someone who has cooked up a fiendish plot and succeeded, although it always sounded like the laughter of someone who has just told an excellent joke. Because he was laughing over the scratchy intercom, Mattathias sounded as if he had a piece of aluminum foil over his mouth, but the laughter was still loud enough to help wear off the anesthesia, and Violet murmured something and moved her arms.

'Oops,' Mattathias said, interrupting his laughter as he realized the intercom was on. 'This is Mattathias, the Head of Human Resources, with an important announcement. There is a terrible fire in Heimlich Hospital. The fire was set in the Library of Records by the Baudelaire murderers, and has spread to the Sore Throat Ward, the Stubbed Toe Ward, and the Accidentally Swallowed Something You Shouldn't Have Ward. The orphans are still at large, so do everything you can to find them. After the murdering arsonists have been captured, you might want to rescue some of the patients who are trapped in the fire. That is all.'

'I can see the headline now,' the reporter said. 'BAUDELAIRE MURDERERS TORCH PAPER-WORK.' Wait until the readers of *The Daily Punctilio* see this!'

'Somebody tell Mattathias we've captured the children,' a nurse cried in triumph. 'You three brats are in big trouble. You're murderers, arsonists, and spurious doctors.'

'That's not true,' Klaus said, but as he looked around he feared that no one would believe him. He looked at the spurious key ring in Hal's hands, that he and his siblings had used to sneak into the Library of Records. He looked at his medical coat, which he had used to disguise himself as a doctor. And he looked at the rusty blade in his own hands, which he had just been holding over his sister. Klaus remembered when he and his sisters were living with Uncle Monty, and brought several objects to Mr. Poe as evidence of Olaf's treacherous plot.

Because of these small objects, Olaf was placed under arrest, and now Klaus was afraid that the same thing would happen to the Baudelaires.

'Surround them!' the hook-handed man called, pointing at the children with one curved glove. 'But be careful. The bookworm still has the knife!' Olaf's associates spread out in a circle and slowly began walking toward the youngsters at all angles. Sunny whimpered in fright, and Klaus picked her up and put her on the gurney.

'Arrest the Baudelaires!' a doctor cried.

'That's what we're doing, you fool!' Esmé replied impatiently, but when she turned her head to the Baudelaires they saw her wink above her surgical mask.

'We're going to capture only one of you,' she said, in a quiet voice so the audience wouldn't hear her. With two long fingernailed hands she reached down to her stiletto heels. 'This in footwear isn't just useful for making me look glamorous and feminine,' she said, removing the shoes and pointing them at the children. 'These stilettos are perfect for slitting children's throats. Two bratty little Baudelaires will be killed while trying to escape from justice, leaving one bratty little Baudelaire to give us the fortune.'

'You'll never get your hands on our fortune,' Klaus said, 'or your shoes on our throats.'

'We'll see,' Esmé said, and swung her left shoe at Klaus as if it were a sword. Klaus ducked quickly and felt the *whoosh!* of air as the blade swept over him.

'She's trying to kill us!' Klaus shouted to the audience. 'Can't you see? These are the real murderers!'

'No one will ever believe you,' Esmé said in a sinister whisper, and swung her right shoe at Sunny, who moved away just in time.

'I don't believe you!' shouted Hal. 'My eyesight might not be what it used to be, but I can see your phony medical coat.'

'I don't believe you, either!' a nurse cried. 'I can see that rusty knife!'

Esmé swung both shoes at the same

time, but they collided in midair instead of hitting the children. 'Why don't you surrender?' she hissed. 'We've finally trapped you, just as you trapped Olaf all those other times.'

'Now you know what it feels like to be a villain,' the bald man chuckled. 'Move closer, everyone! Mattathias told me that whoever grabs them first gets to choose where to go for dinner tonight!'

'Is that so?' the hook-handed man asked. 'Well, I'm in the mood for pizza.' He swung a rubber-gloved hook at Klaus, who fell back against the gurney, rolling it out of the evil man's reach.

'I feel more like Chinese food,' one of the powder-faced women said. 'Let's go to that place where we celebrated the Quagmire kidnapping.'

'I want to go to Cafe Salmonella,' Esmé snarled, disentangling her shoes.

Klaus pushed against the gurney again, wheeling it in the other direction as the circle of associates closed in. He held the rusty knife up for protection, but the middle Baudelaire did not think he could use a weapon, even on people as wicked as these. If Count Olaf had been trapped, he would not have hesitated to swing the rusty blade at the people who were surrounding him, but despite what the bald man had said, Klaus did not feel like a villain. He felt like someone who needed to escape, and as he pushed against the gurney again, he knew how he was going to do it.

'Get back!' Klaus cried. 'This knife is very sharp!'

'You can't kill all of us,' the hook-handed man replied. 'In fact, I doubt you have the courage to kill anyone.'

'It doesn't take courage to kill someone,' Klaus said. 'It takes a severe lack of moral stamina.'

At the mention of the phrase 'severe lack of moral stamina,' which here means 'cruel selfishness combined with a love of violence,' Olaf's associates laughed in delight. 'Your fancy words won't save you now, you twerp,' Esmé said.

'That's true,' Klaus admitted. 'What will save me now is a bed on wheels used to transport hospital patients.'

Without another word, Klaus tossed the rusty knife to the floor, startling Olaf's associates into stepping back. The circle of people with a severe lack of moral stamina was spread out a little more, just for a moment, but a moment was all the Baudelaires needed. Klaus jumped onto the gurney, which began to roll quickly toward the square metal door they had come in. A cry rose from the audience as the Baudelaires sped past Olaf's associates.

'Get them!' the hook-handed man cried. 'They're getting away!'

'They won't get away from me!' Hal promised, and grabbed the gurney just before it reached the door. The gurney slowed to a halt, and for a second Sunny found herself face-to-face with the old man. Butterflies fluttered in the youngest Baudelaire's stomach as he glared at her from behind his tiny glasses. Unlike Olaf's associates, Hal was not an evil person, of course. He was merely someone who loved the Library of Records and was trying to capture the people he believed had set it on fire, and it pained Sunny to see that he thought she was an evil criminal, instead of an unlucky infant. But she knew she did not have time to explain to Hal what had really happened. She scarcely had time to say a single word, and yet that is precisely what the youngest Baudelaire did.

'Sorry,' Sunny said to Hal, and gave him a small smile. Then she opened her mouth a little wider, and bit Hal's hand as gently as she could, so that he would let go of the gurney without getting hurt.

'Ow!' Hal said, and let go. 'The baby bit me!' he shouted to the crowd.

'Are you hurt?' a nurse asked.

'No,' Hal replied, 'but I let go of the gurney. They're rolling out the door!'

The Baudelaires rolled out the door, with Violet's eyes flickering open, Klaus steering the gurney, and Sunny hanging on for dear life. The children rolled down the hallways of the Surgical Ward, dodging around surprised doctors and other medical professionals.

'Attention!' announced Mattathias's

voice over the intercom. 'This is Mattathias, the Head of Human Resources! The Baudelaire murderers and arsonists are escaping on a gurney! Capture them at once! Also, the fire is spreading throughout the hospital! You might want to evacuate!'

'Noriz!' Sunny shouted.

'I'm going as fast as I can!' Klaus cried, dangling his legs over the side of the gurney to scoot it along. 'Violet, wake up, please! You can help push!'

'I'm try . . . ing . . .' Violet muttered, squinting around her. The anesthesia made everything seem faint and foggy, and it was almost impossible for her to speak, let alone move.

'Door!' Sunny shrieked, pointing to the door that led out of the Surgical Ward. Klaus steered the gurney in that direction and rode past Olaf's fat associate who looked like neither a man nor a woman, who was still dressed as a spurious guard. With a terrible roar, it began to give chase, walking in huge, lumbering steps, as the Baudelaires raced toward a small group of Volunteers Fighting Disease.

208

The bearded volunteer, who was playing some very familiar chords on his guitar, looked up to see the gurney wheel past them.

'Those must be those murderers Mattathias was talking about!' he said. 'Come on, everyone, let's help that guard capture them!'

'Sounds good to me,' another volunteer agreed. 'I'm a bit tired of singing that song, if you want to know the truth.'

Klaus steered the gurney around a corner, as the volunteers joined the overweight associate in pursuit. 'Wake up,' he begged Violet, who was looking around her in a confused way. 'Please, Violet!'

'Stairs!' Sunny said, pointing to a staircase. Klaus turned the gurney in the direction his sister indicated, and the children began to roll down the stairs, bouncing up and down with each step. It was a fast, slippery ride that reminded the children of sliding down the bannisters at 667 Dark Avenue, or colliding with Mr. Poe's automobile when they were living with Uncle

Monty. At a curve in the staircase, Klaus scraped his shoes against the floor to stop the gurney, and then leaned over to look at one of the hospital's confusing maps.

'I'm trying to figure out if we should go through that door,' he said, pointing at a door marked 'Ward for People with Nasty Rashes,' 'or continue down the staircase.'

'Dleen!' Sunny cried, which meant 'We can't continue down the staircase —look!'

Klaus looked, and even Violet managed to focus enough to look down where Sunny was pointing. Down the staircase, just past the next landing, was a flickering, orange glow, as if the sun was rising out of the hospital basement, and a few wisps of dark black smoke were curling up the staircase like the tentacles of some ghostly animal. It was an eerie sight that had haunted the Baudelaires in their dreams, ever since that fateful day at the beach when all their trouble began. For a moment, the three children were unable to do anything but stare down at the orange glow and the tentacles of smoke, and think about all they had lost because of what they were looking at.

'Fire,' Violet said faintly.

'Yes,' Klaus said. 'It's spreading up this staircase. We've got to turn and go back upstairs.'

From upstairs, the Baudelaires listened to the associate roar again, and heard the bearded volunteer reply.

'We'll help you capture them,' he said. 'Lead the way, sir—or is it madam? I can't tell.'

'No up,' Sunny said.

'I know,' Klaus said. 'We can't go up the stairs and we can't go down. We have to go into the Ward for People with Nasty Rashes.'

Having made this rash decision, Klaus turned the gurney and wheeled it through the door, just as Mattathias's voice came through on the intercom. 'This is Mattathias, the Head of Human Resources,' he said hurriedly. 'All associates of Dr. Flacutono, continue to search for the children! Everyone else, gather in front of the hospital—either we will catch the murderers as they escape, or they'll be burned to a crisp!'

The children rolled into the Ward for People with Nasty Rashes and saw that Mattathias was right. The gurney was racing down a hallway, and the children could see another orange glow at the far end of it. The children heard another roar behind them as the overweight associate lumbered down the stairs. The siblings were trapped in the middle of a hallway that led only to a fiery death or to Olaf's clutches.

Klaus leaned down and stopped the gurney. 'We'd better hide,' he said, jumping to the floor. 'It's too dangerous to be rolling around like this.'

'Where?' Sunny asked, as Klaus helped her down.

'Someplace close by,' Klaus said, grabbing Violet's arm. 'The anesthesia is still wearing off, so Violet can't walk too far.'

'I'll . . . try . . .' Violet murmured, stepping unsteadily off the gurney and leaning on Klaus. The children looked around and saw that the nearest door was marked 'Supply Closet.'

'Glaynop?' Sunny asked.

'I guess so,' Klaus said doubtfully, opening the door with one hand while balancing Violet with the other. 'I don't know what we can do in a supply closet, but at least it'll hide us for a few moments.'

Klaus and Sunny helped their sister through the door and locked it behind them. Except for a small window in the corner, the closet looked identical to the one where Klaus and Sunny had hidden to decipher the anagram in the patient list. It was a small room, with only one flickering lightbulb hanging from the ceiling, and there was a row of white medical coats hanging from hooks, a rusty sink, huge cans of alphabet soup, and small boxes of rubber bands, but as the two younger Baudelaires looked at these supplies, they did not look like devices for translating anagrams and impersonating medical professionals. Klaus and Sunny looked at all these objects, and then at their older sister. To their relief, Violet's face was a bit less pale, and her eyes were a bit less confused, which was a very good sign. The eldest Baudelaire needed to be as awake as she could be, because the items in the closet were looking less and less like supplies, and more and more like materials for an invention.

CHAPTER THIRTEEN

When Violet Baudelaire was five years old, she won her first invention contest with an automatic rolling pin she'd fashioned out of a broken window shade and six pairs of roller skates. As the judges placed the gold medal around her neck, one of them said to her, 'I bet you could invent something with both hands tied behind your back,' and Violet smiled proudly. She knew, of course, that the judge did not mean that he was going to tie her up, but merely that she was so skilled at inventing that she could probably build something even with substantial interference, a phrase which here means 'something getting in her way.'

The eldest Baudelaire had proved the judge right dozens of times, of course, inventing everything from a lockpick to a welding torch with the substantial interference of being in a hurry and not having the right tools. But Violet thought she had never had as much substantial interference as the lingering effects of anesthesia as she squinted at the objects in the supply closet and tried to focus on what her siblings were saying.

'Violet,' Klaus said, 'I know that the anesthesia hasn't completely worn off, but we need you to try to invent something.'

'Yes,' Violet said faintly, rubbing her eyes with her hands. 'I . . . know.'

'We'll help you all we can,' Klaus said. 'Just tell us what to do. The fire is consuming this entire hospital, and we have to get out of here quickly.'

'Rallam,' Sunny added, which meant 'And Olaf's associates are chasing us.'

'Open . . . the window,' Violet said with difficulty, pointing to the window in the corner.

Klaus helped Violet lean against the wall, so he could step over to the window without letting her fall. He opened the window and looked outside. 'It looks like we're on the third floor,' he said, 'or maybe the fourth. There's smoke in the air, so it's hard to tell. We're not so high up, but it's still too far to jump.'

'Climb?' Sunny asked.

'There's an intercom speaker right below us,' Klaus said. 'I suppose we could hang on to that and climb down to the bushes below, but we'd be climbing in front of a huge crowd. The doctors and nurses are helping the patients escape, and there's Hal, and that reporter from *The Daily Punctilio* and—'

The middle Baudelaire was interrupted by a faint sound coming from outside the hospital.

'We are Volunteers Fighting Disease,
And we're cheerful all day long.

217

If someone said that we were sad,
That person would be wrong.'

'And the Volunteers Fighting Disease,' Klaus continued. 'They're waiting at the entrance to the hospital, just like Mattathias told them to. Can you invent something to fly over them?'

Violet frowned and closed her eyes, standing still for a moment as the volunteers continued singing.

'We visit people who are sick,
And try to make them smile,
Even if their noses bleed,
Or if they cough up bile.'

'Violet?' Klaus asked. 'You're not falling asleep again, are you?'

'No,' Violet said. 'I'm . . . thinking. We need . . . to distract . . . the crowd . . . before we . . . climb down.'

The children heard a faint roar from beyond the closet door. 'Kesalf,' Sunny said, which meant 'That's Olaf's associate. It sounds like it's entering the Ward for People with Nasty Rashes. We'd better hurry.'

'Klaus,' Violet said, and opened her eyes. 'Open those boxes . . . of rubber bands. Start to string . . . them together . . . to make . . . a cord.'

> *'Tra la la, Fiddle dee dee,*
> *Hope you get well soon.*
> *Ho ho ho, hee hee hee,*
> *Have a heart-shaped balloon.'*

Klaus looked down and watched the volunteers giving balloons out to the hospital patients who had been evacuated from the hospital. 'But how will we distract the crowd?' he asked.

'I . . . don't know,' Violet admitted, and looked down at the floor. 'I'm having . . . trouble focusing my . . . inventing skills.'

'Help,' Sunny said.

'Don't cry for help, Sunny,' Klaus said. 'No one will hear us.'

'Help,' Sunny insisted, and took off her white medical coat. Opening her mouth wide, she bit down on the fabric, ripping a small strip off the coat with her teeth. Then she held up the strip of white cloth, and handed it to Violet.

'Ribbon,' she said, and Violet gave her a weary smile. With unsteady fingers, the eldest Baudelaire tied her hair up to keep it out of her eyes, using the thin strip of fabric instead of a hair ribbon. She closed her eyes again, and then nodded.

'I know . . . it's a bit silly,' Violet said. 'I think . . . it did help, Sunny. Klaus . . . get to work . . . on the rubber bands. Sunny—can you open . . . one of those cans of soup?'

'Treen,' Sunny said, which meant 'Yes—I opened one earlier, to help decode the anagrams.'

'Good,' Violet replied. With her hair up in a ribbon—even if the ribbon was spurious—her voice sounded stronger and more confident. 'We need . . . an empty can . . . as quickly as . . . possible.'

'We visit people who are ill,
And try to make them laugh,
Even when the doctor says
He must saw them in half.

220

We sing and sing all night and day,
And then we sing some more.
We sing to boys with broken bones
And girls whose throats are sore.'

As the members of V.F.D. continued their cheerful song, the Baudelaires worked quickly. Klaus opened a box of rubber bands and began stringing them together, Sunny began to gnaw at the top of a can of soup, and Violet went to the sink and splashed water on her face to try to make herself as alert as possible. Finally, by the time the volunteers were singing

'Tra la la, Fiddle dee dee,
Hope you get well soon.
Ho ho ho, hee hee hee,
Have a heart-shaped balloon.'

Klaus had a long cord of rubber bands curled at his feet like a snake, Sunny had taken the top off a can of soup and was pouring it down the sink, and Violet was staring anxiously at the bottom of the closet door, from which a very thin wisp of smoke was crawling out.

'The fire is in the hallway,' Violet said, as the children heard another roar from the hallway, 'and so is Olaf's henchperson. We have only a few moments.'

'The cord is all ready,' Klaus said, 'but how can we distract the crowd with an empty soup can?'

'It's not an empty soup can,' Violet said, 'not anymore. Now it's a spurious intercom. Sunny, poke one hole in the bottom of the can.'

'Pietrisycamollaviadelrechiotemexity,' Sunny said, but she did as Violet asked and poked her sharpest tooth through the bottom of the can.

'Now,' Violet said, 'you two hold this near the window. Don't let the crowd see it. They have to think my voice is coming out of the intercom.'

Klaus and Sunny held the empty soup can near the window, and Violet leaned in and stuck her head inside it, as if it were a mask. The eldest Baudelaire took a deep breath to gather her courage, and then she began to speak. From inside the can her voice sounded scratchy and faint, as if she were talking with a piece of aluminum foil over her mouth, which was precisely how she wanted to sound.

'Attention!' Violet announced, before the volunteers could sing the verse about singing to men with measles. 'This is Babs. Mattathias has resigned due to personal problems, so I am once again the Head of Human Resources. The Baudelaire murderers and arsonists have been spotted in the unfinished wing of the hospital. We require everyone's assistance in making sure they do not escape. Please rush over there right away. That is all.'

Violet pulled her head out of the can, and looked at her siblings. 'Do you think it worked?' she asked.

Sunny opened her mouth to answer, but she was interrupted by the voice of the bearded volunteer.

'Did you hear that?' the children heard him say. 'The criminals are over in the unfinished half of the hospital. Come on, everyone.'

'Maybe some of us should stay here at the front entrance, just in case,' said a voice the Baudelaires recognized as Hal's.

Violet stuck her head back into the can. 'Attention!' she announced. 'This is Babs, the Head of Human Resources. No one should stay at the front entrance to the hospital. It's too dangerous. Proceed at once to the unfinished wing. That is all.'

'I can see the headline now,' said the reporter from *The Daily Punctilio*. '"MURDERERS CAPTURED IN UNFINISHED HALF OF HOSPITAL BY WELL-ORGANIZED MEDICAL PROFESSIONALS." Wait until the readers of *The Daily Punctilio* see that!'

There was a cheer from the crowd, which faded as they walked away from the front of Heimlich Hospital.

'It worked,' Violet said. 'We fooled them. We're as good at tricking people as Olaf is.'

'And at disguises,' Klaus said.

'Anagrams,' Sunny said.

'And lying to people,' Violet said, thinking of Hal, and the shopkeeper at Last Chance General Store and all the Volunteers Fighting Disease. 'Maybe we're becoming villains after all.'

'Don't say that,' Klaus said. 'We're not villains. We're good people. We had to do tricky things in order to save our lives.'

'Olaf has to do tricky things,' Violet said, 'to save his life.'

'Different,' Sunny said.

'Maybe it's not different,' Violet said sadly. 'Maybe—'

Violet was interrupted by an angry roar coming from just outside the closet door. Olaf's overweight assistant had reached the supply closet and was now fumbling at the door with its enormous hands.

'We can discuss this later,' Klaus said. 'We have to get out of here right now.'

'We're not going to climb,' Violet said, 'not with such a skinny, rubbery cord. We're going to bounce.'

'Bounce?' Sunny asked doubtfully.

'Plenty of people bounce from high places on long, rubbery cords just for fun,' Violet said, 'so I'm sure we can do it to escape. I'll tie the cord to the faucet with the Devil's Tongue knot,

225

and we'll each take turns jumping out the window. The cord should catch us before we hit the ground, and bounce us up, and down, and up, and down, more and more gently each time. Eventually we'll get to the bottom safely, and then we'll toss it back up to the next person.'

'It sounds risky,' Klaus said. 'I'm not sure the cord is long enough.'

'It is risky,' Violet agreed, 'but not as risky as a fire.'

The associate rattled the door furiously, making a large crack right near the lock. Black smoke began to pour through the crack as if the assistant were pouring ink into the closet, as Violet hurriedly tied the cord to the faucet and then tugged on it to make sure it was secure.

'I'll go first,' she said. 'I invented it, so I'd better test it.'

'No,' Klaus said. 'We're not taking turns.'

'Together,' Sunny agreed.

'If we all go down together,' Violet said, 'I'm not sure the cord will hold.'

'We're not leaving anyone behind,'

226

Klaus said firmly. 'Not this time. Either we all escape, or none of us do.'

'But if none of us do,' Violet said tearfully, 'then there won't be any Baudelaires left. Olaf will have won.'

Klaus reached into his pocket and brought out a sheet of paper. He unfolded it, and his sisters could see that it was page thirteen of the Snicket file. He pointed to the photograph of the Baudelaire parents and the sentence that was printed below it. ' "Because of the evidence discussed on page nine",' he read out loud, ' "experts now suspect that there may in fact be one survivor of the fire, but the survivor's whereabouts are unknown." We've got to survive, too—so we can find out what happened, and bring Olaf to justice.'

'But if we take turns,' Violet said frantically, 'there's a better chance that one of us will survive.'

'We're not leaving anyone behind,' Klaus said firmly. 'That's what makes us different from Olaf.'

Violet thought for a moment, and nodded. 'You're right,' she said.

Olaf's associate kicked at the door, and the crack grew bigger. The children could see a tiny orange light shining in the hallway and realized that the fire and the associate must have reached the door at the same time.

'I'm scared,' Violet said.

'I'm frightened,' Klaus said.

'Sheer terror,' Sunny said, and the associate kicked the door again, forcing a few sparks through the crack in the door. The Baudelaires looked at one another, and each child grabbed the rubber band cord with one hand. With their other hands they clasped one another, and then, without another word, they leaped out of the window of Heimlich Hospital

STOP.

There are many things in this world I do not know. I do not know how butterflies get out of their cocoons without damaging their wings. I do not know why anyone would boil vegetables when roasting them is tastier. I do not know how to make olive oil, and I do not know why dogs bark before an earthquake, and I do not know why some people voluntarily choose to climb mountains where it is freezing and difficult to breathe, or live in the suburbs, where the coffee is watery and all of the houses look alike. I do not know where the Baudelaire children are now, or if they are safe or if they are even alive. But there are some things I do know, and one of them is that the window of the supply closet in the Ward for People with Nasty Rashes of Heimlich Hospital was not on the third floor or the fourth floor, as Klaus had guessed. The window was on the second floor, so that when the three children dropped through the smoky air, clinging to the rubber band cord for dear life, Violet's invention worked perfectly. Like a yo-yo, the children bounced gently up and down, brushing their feet against one of the bushes planted in front of the hospital, and after a few bounces it was safe to drop to the ground and hug each other with relief.

'We made it,' Violet said. 'It was a close call, but we survived.'

The Baudelaires looked behind them at the hospital, and saw just how close a call it had been. The building looked like a fiery ghost, with great bursts of flame coming from the windows, and oceans of smoke pouring from great gaping holes in the walls. The children could hear glass shattering as the windows burned away, and the crackle of wood as the floors fell through. It occurred to the children that their own house must have looked like this on the day it burned down, and they stepped back from the burning building and huddled together as the air grew thick with ashes and smoke, obscuring the hospital from view.

'Where can we go?' Klaus asked, shouting over the roar of the fire. 'Any minute now, the crowd will figure out that we're not in the unfinished half of the hospital, and return here.'

'Run!' Sunny shrieked.

'But we can't even see where we're going!' Violet cried. 'The whole area is filling up with smoke!'

'Stay down!' Klaus said, dropping to the ground and beginning to crawl. 'In *The Encyclopedia of Escaping Arson*, the author wrote that there's more oxygen closer to the ground, so we can breathe more easily. But we need to get to some kind of shelter right away.'

'Where will we find some kind of shelter, in this empty landscape?' Violet asked, crawling behind her brother. 'The hospital is the only building for miles, and it's burning to the ground!'

'I don't know,' Klaus said, coughing loudly, 'but we can't breathe in this smoke for long!'

'Hurry up!' the Baudelaires heard a voice call out of the smoke. 'This way!' A long, black shape emerged from the smoky air, and the children saw it was an automobile, pulling up in front of the hospital. An automobile, of course, is a kind of shelter, but the siblings froze on the ground and dared not crawl an inch farther toward the car.

'Hurry up!' Olaf's voice said again. 'Hurry up or I'll leave you behind!'

231

'I'm coming, darling.' From behind them, the Baudelaires heard the reply of Esmé Squalor. 'Lucafont and Flacutono are with me, and the ladies are following behind. I had them take all the medical coats we could find, in case we need them for costumes again.'

'Good thinking,' Olaf replied. 'Can you see the car in the smoke?'

'Yes,' Esmé said, her voice growing closer. The Baudelaires could hear the odd footsteps of her stiletto-heeled shoes as she strode toward the automobile. 'Open the trunk, darling, and we'll put the costumes in.'

'Oh, all right,' Olaf sighed, and the children saw the tall figure of their enemy step out of the car.

'Wait up, Olaf!' the bald man cried.

'You fool,' Olaf replied. 'I told you to call me Mattathias until we leave the hospital grounds. Hurry up and get in the car. The Snicket file wasn't in the Library of Records, but I think I know where I can find it. Once we destroy those thirteen pages, there'll be no stopping us.'

'We've got to destroy the

Baudelaires, too,' Esmé said.

'We would have destroyed them, if all of you hadn't messed up my plan,' he said, 'but never mind that. We have to get out of here before the authorities come.'

'But your largest assistant is still in the Rash Ward, looking for the brats!' the bald man said, and the children heard him open the door of the automobile.

The hook-handed man spoke up, and the children could see his odd shape in the smoke as he got into the car after the bald assistant. 'The Ward for People with Nasty Rashes is entirely destroyed,' he said. 'I hope the big one got out O.K.'

'We're not going to wait around to find out if that fool lived or died,' Olaf snarled. 'As soon as the ladies can put the costumes in the trunk, we'll get out of here. It's been splendid setting this fire, but we've got to find the Snicket file as soon as possible, before You-Know-Who does.'

'V.F.D.!' Esmé said with a cackle. 'The *real* V.F.D., that is, not those ridiculous singers!'

The trunk opened with a creak, and the children saw the shadow of the trunk's lid flip open into the smoky air. The lid was peppered with tiny holes—bullet holes, it looked like, undoubtedly from being pursued by the police. Olaf strode back to the car and continued giving orders.

'Get out of the front seat, you idiots,' Olaf said. 'My girlfriend sits in front, and the rest of you can pile in the back.'

'Yes, boss,' the bald man replied.

'We have the costumes, Mattathias.' The voice of one of the powder-faced women was faint in the smoke. 'Just give us a few seconds to reach the car.'

Violet leaned as close as she could to her siblings so she could whisper to them without being heard. 'We've got to go in there,' she said.

'Where?' Klaus whispered in reply.

'In the trunk,' Violet replied. 'It's our only chance to get out of here without getting captured—or worse.'

'Culech!' Sunny said in a horrified whisper, which meant something along the lines of 'Getting in the trunk is the same thing as getting captured!'

'We've got to get the rest of the Snicket file before Olaf does,' Violet said, 'or we'll never be able to clear our names.'

'Or bring Olaf to justice,' Klaus said.

'Ezan,' Sunny said, which meant 'Or find out if one of our parents really survived the fire.'

'The only way we can do all those things,' Violet said, 'is to get in the trunk of that car.'

Olaf's voice floated through the smoke, as deceitful and dangerous as the fire itself. 'Get in the car this instant!' he ordered his associates. 'I'm going to leave at the count of three.'

The Baudelaires gripped each other's hands so firmly that it hurt to hang on. 'Think of everything we have survived together,' Violet whispered. 'We've lived through countless unfortunate events, only to find ourselves alone. If one of our parents has survived, it'll all be worthwhile. We have to find them if it's the last thing we do.'

'One!'

Klaus looked at the gaping trunk, which looked like the mouth of some dark and smoky beast, eager to devour him and his siblings. 'You're right,' he murmured finally. 'We can't stay in this smoky air much longer, or we'll become asphyxiated. The shelter of the trunk is our only hope.'

'Yes!' Sunny whispered.

'Two!'

The Baudelaire children stood up and scurried into the trunk of Count Olaf's car. The trunk was damp and smelled terrible, but the children crawled deep into its depths so they wouldn't be seen.

'Wait!' the powder-faced woman called, and the Baudelaires felt the slap of the medical coats being tossed on top of them. 'I don't want to be left behind! I can't breathe out here!'

'Will we be able to breathe in here?' Violet asked Klaus as quietly as she could.

'Yes,' Klaus said. 'Air will come through the bullet holes. This is not the sort of shelter I had in mind, but I

236

guess it might do.'

'Golos,' Sunny said, which meant 'It'll have to do, until something better comes along,' and her siblings nodded.

'Three!'

The trunk slammed closed, leaving them in utter darkness, and their shelter rattled and shook as Olaf started the engine and began to drive across the landscape, which was as flat and desolate as ever. But the children could not see outside, of course. In the blackness of the trunk, they could not see anything at all. They could only hear their long, shivering breaths as the air rushed through the bullet holes, and feel their shoulders tremble as they shivered in fear. It was not the sort of shelter the children had in mind, never in their entire lives, but as they huddled together they guessed it might do. For the Baudelaire orphans—if indeed they were still orphans—the shelter of Count Olaf's trunk would have to do, until something better came along.

© Meredith Hever

LEMONY SNICKET is widely regarded as one of the most difficult children's authors to capture and imprison. Recently, he had to give up his hobbies due to laws regarding musical performances in mountainous terrain. Most things written about him are not true, but this is.

www.unfortunateevents.com

BRETT HELQUIST was born in Ganado, Arizona, grew up in Orem, Utah, and now lives in New York City, where among other noble pursuits, he translates Mr Snicket's obscure findings into the images that help readers understand the horror of the Baudelaires' plight.

To My Kind Editor,

I hope that this letter is not mangled by the
ferocious and deadly ....
.... in which I am hiding now.
.... thirteen hundred
nineteen and one-half miles (DOOBY kilometers)
from the restaurant where you celebrated your
most recent birthday ....

.... may then exchange (at a near laundromat
or jewelry store) for ....
....

...... with ... a long mustache. She will give you
the complete manuscript of THE CARNIVOROUS CAR-
NIVAL, along with a satchel containi..............
.... --which under no
circumstances should you repair-- ....

he last .... survivor of the Baude..

.... a sketch
of Chabo, the Wolf Baby, and Madame Lulu
.... or, at least, what is left o...

Remember, you are my last hope that the tales of
the Baudelaire orphans can finally be told to the
general public.

        With all due respect,

        Lemony Snicket

        Lemony Snicket